EARLIER AMERICAN MUSIC

EDITED BY H. WILEY HITCHCOCK
for the *Music Library Association*

11

THE INDIAN PRINCESS

THE INDIAN PRINCESS

or

La Belle Sauvage

An Operatic Melo-Drame in Three Acts

Text by James Nelson Barker

Music by John Bray

New Introduction by H. Wiley Hitchcock
Director, Institute for Studies in American Music,
Brooklyn College, CUNY

DA CAPO PRESS • NEW YORK • 1972

This Da Capo Press edition of *The Indian Princess* combines in one volume John Bray's score, published originally in Philadelphia in 1808, and the complete text of James Nelson Barker's drama, also first published in Philadelphia in 1808. The text section is reproduced with permission from a copy of the original edition in the Library of the University of North Carolina.

Library of Congress Catalog Card Number 77-169587

ISBN 0-306-77311-2

Copyright © 1972 by the Music Library Association

Published by Da Capo Press Inc.
A Subsidiary of Plenum Publishing Corporation
227 West 17th Street, New York, New York 10011

Manufactured in the United States of America

EDITOR'S FOREWORD

American musical culture, from Colonial and Federal Era days on, has been reflected in an astonishing production of printed music of all kinds: by 1820, for instance, more than fifteen thousand musical publications had issued from American presses. Fads, fashions, and tastes have changed so rapidly in our history, however, that comparatively little earlier American music has remained in print. On the other hand, the past few decades have seen an explosion of interest in earlier American culture, including earlier American music. College and university courses in American civilization and American music have proliferated; recording companies have found a surprising response to earlier American composers and their music; a wave of interest in folk and popular music of past eras has opened up byways of musical experience unimagined only a short time ago.

It seems an opportune moment, therefore, to make available for study and enjoyment—and as an aid to furthering performance of earlier American music—works of significance that exist today only in a few scattered copies of publications long out of print, and works that may be well known only in later editions or arrangements having little relationship to the original compositions.

Earlier American Music is planned around several types of musical scores to be reprinted from early editions of the eighteenth, nineteenth, and early twentieth centuries. The categories are as follows:

> Songs and other solo vocal music
> Choral music and part-songs
> Solo keyboard music
> Chamber music
> Orchestral music and concertos
> Dance music and marches for band
> Theater music

The idea of *Earlier American Music* originated in a paper read before the Music Library Association in February, 1968, and published under the title "A Monumenta Americana?" in the Association's journal, *Notes* (September, 1968). It seems most appropriate, therefore, for the Music Library Association to sponsor this series. We hope *Earlier American Music* will stimulate further study and performance of musical Americana.

H. Wiley Hitchcock

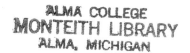

INTRODUCTION

Operas were staged in the American colonies beginning in the 1730's—not the elaborate and aristocratic Baroque operas of continental Europe but English "ballad operas." These were the plays-with-songs that had begun with John Gay's *Beggar's Opera* of 1728, a tale of London's underworld satirizing the political and social establishment. (Kurt Weill's *Dreigroschenoper* and Marc Blitzstein's adaptation of it, *The Three-Penny Opera,* are based on Gay's original.) The music of the early ballad operas consisted simply of folk and popular tunes set to new texts; later in the eighteenth century, modest but newly-composed airs and choruses found their way into them.

The Indian Princess, first played at the Chestnut Street Theatre in Philadelphia, April 6, 1808, comes out of the English ballad-opera tradition. In addition, however (and this is one of its major points of interest), it includes descriptive incidental music of the sort to be heard in French and German "melodrama" of the time, the term then denoting a play with background music for instruments. This explains the subtitle of the play, "an operatic melo-drame."

James Nelson Barker's play is of interest as the work of an early nativist playwright (as opposed to those, like John Howard Payne, who eschewed American subject matter), and as the earliest surviving play on the story of Captain John Smith and Pocahontas. The music, by the British-born actor-translator-composer, John Bray (1782–1822), is of interest partly because of its very existence: seldom was the entire musical score of a ballad opera published, instead usually only the "hit songs." In this instance, the music was published complete, but separate from the play; our reprint edition brings the two together for the first time.

Barker (1784–1858) had no illusions about the artistic stature of his play. In his preface he admits that in America "every art is yet but in its infancy," and he refers to *The Indian Princess* as a "little piece [with] very humble merit. . . . 'Tis a plain-palated, home-bred, and I may add independent urchin." Bray might well have agreed with this estimate in evaluating his music. A couple of the airs are rather amusing, and at least Pocahontas' "When the midnight of absence" has a modicum of graceful lyricism. Otherwise, the music too has "humble merit"—but it is not lacking in entertainment value, especially when heard with the play. The snippets of background mood music, open-ended, to be repeated as many times as necessary during a given scene, heighten the light sentimentality of the drama (this was the era, after all, of Richardson's *Pamela* and Susanna Rowan's *Charlotte Temple: A Tale of Truth*). They point to the exaggerated emotionalism of later American drama ("melodrama" in another sense), and they foreshadow later American background music for dramas and films.

A more extended discussion of *The Indian Princess* than is possible here will be found in H. W. Hitchcock, "An Early American Melodrama," *Notes,* XII (1955), 375-88.

H.W.H.

THE INDIAN PRINCESS

Text

THE

INDIAN PRINCESS;

OR,

LA BELLE SAUVAGE.

AN OPERATIC MELO-DRAME.

IN THREE ACTS.

PERFORMED AT THE THEATRES PHILADELPHIA AND
BALTIMORE.

———

BY J. N. BARKER.

———

FIRST ACTED APRIL 6, 1808.

━━━━━━

PHILADELPHIA,

PRINTED BY T. & G. PALMER,

FOR G. E. BLAKE, NO. 1, SOUTH THIRD-STREET,

. . . .

1808.

PREFACE.

WHILE I am proud to acknowledge my grateful sense of those flattering marks of liberal kindness with which my dramatic entree has been greeted by an indulgent audience, I feel so fully conscious of the very humble merit of this little piece, that perhaps nothing but the peculiar circumstances under which it was acted should have induced me to publish it. In sending it to the press I am perfectly apprized of the probability that it goes only to add one more to the list of those unfortunate children of the American drama, who, in the brief space that lies between their birth and death, are doomed to wander, without house or home, unknown and unregarded, or who, if heeded at all, are only picked up by some critic beadle to receive the usual treatment of vagrants. Indeed, were I disposed to draw comfort from the misfortunes of others, I might make myself happy with the reflection, that however my vagabond might deserve the lash, it would receive no more punishment than those who deserved none at all; for the gentlemen castigators seldom take the pains to distinguish Innocence from Guilt, but most liberally bestow their stripes on all poor wanderers who are unhappily of American parentage. Far, however, from rejoicing at this circumstance, I sincerely deplore it. In all ages, and in every country, even the sturdiest offspring of genius have felt the necessity and received the aid of a protecting hand of favour to support and guide their first trembling and devious footsteps; it is not, therefore, wonderful, that here, where every art is yet but in its infancy, the youthful exertions of dramatic poetry, unaided and unsupported, should fail, and that its imbecile efforts should for ever cease with the failure; that chilled by total neglect, or chid with undeserved severity; depressed by ridicule, starved by envy, and stricken to the earth by malevolence, the poor orphan, heartless and spirit-broken, should pine away a short and sickly life. I am not, I believe, quite coxcomb enough to advance the most distant hint that the child of my brain deserves a better fate; that it may meet with it I might, however, be indulged in hoping, under the profession that the hope proceeds from considerations distinct from either it or myself. Dramatic genius, with genius of every other kind, is assuredly native of our soil, and there wants but the wholesome and kindly breath of favour to invigorate its delicate frame, and bid it rapidly arise from its cradle to blooming maturity. But alas! poor weak ones! what a climate are ye doomed to draw your first breath in! the teeming press has scarcely ceased groaning at your delivery, ere you are suffocated with the stagnant atmosphere of entire apathy, or swept out of existence by the hurricane of unsparing, indiscriminating censure!

Good reader, I begin to suspect that I have held you long enough by the button. Yet, maugre my terror of being tiresome, and in despite of my clear anticipation of the severe puns which will be made in this punning city, on my *childish* preface, I must push my allusion a little further, to deprecate the wrath of the critics, and arouse the sympathies of the ladies. Then, O ye sage censors! ye goody gossips at poetic births! I vehemently importune ye to be convinced, that for my bantling I desire neither rattle nor bells; neither the lullaby of praise, nor the pap of patronage, nor the hobby-horse of honour. 'Tis a plain-palated, home-bred, and I may add independent urchin, who laughs at sugar plumbs, and from its little heart disdains gilded gingerbread. If you like it—so; if not—why so; yet, without being mischievous, it would fain be amusing; therefore, if its gambols be pleasant, and your gravities permit, laugh; if not, e'en turn aside your heads, and let the wanton youngling laugh by itself. If it speak like a sensible child, prithee pat its cheek, and say so; but if it be ridiculous when it would be serious, smile, and permit the foolish attempt to pass. But do not, O goody critic, apply the birch, because its unpractised tongue cannot lisp the language of Shakspeare, nor be very much enraged, if you find it has to creep before it can possibly walk.

To your bosoms, ladies, sweet ladies! the little stranger flies with confidence for protection; shield it, I pray you, from the iron rod of rigour, and scold it yourselves, as much as you will, for on *your* smooth and polished brows it can never read wrinkled cruelty; the mild anger of *your* eyes will not blast it like the fierce scowl of the critic; the chidings of *your* voice will be soothing music to it, and it will discover the dimple of kindness in your very frowns. Caresses it does not ask; its modesty would shrink from that it thought it deserved not; but if its faults be infantile, its punishment should be gentle, and from you, dear ladies, correction would be as thrillingly sweet as that the little *Jean Jacques* received from the fair hand of mademoiselle Lambercier.

THE AUTHOR.

ADVERTISEMENT.

THE principal materials that form this dramatic trifle are extracted from the General History of Virginia, written by captain Smith, and printed London, folio, 1624; and as close an adherence to historic truth has been preserved as dramatic rules would allow of. The music* was furnished by Mr. John Bray, of the New Theatre.

* The music is now published and sold by Mr. G. E. Blake, No. 1, South Third-street, Philadelphia.

DRAMATIS PERSONÆ.

EUROPEANS.

Delawar,	*Mr.* WARREN,
Captain Smith,	RUTHERFORD,
Lieutenant Rolfe,	WOOD,
Percy,	CHARNOCK,
Walter,	BRAY,
Larry,	WEBSTER,
Robin,	JEFFERSON,
Talman,	DURANG.
Geraldine,	*Mrs.* FRANCIS,
Kate,	*Miss* HUNT,
Alice,	*Mrs.* MILLS.

Soldiers and adventurers.

VIRGINIANS.

Powhatan, king,	*Mr.* SERSON,
Nantaquas, his son,	CONE,
Miami, a prince,	MILLS,
Grimosco, a priest,	CROSS.
Pocahontas, the princess,	*Mrs.* WILMOT,
Nima, her atttendant,	*Miss* MULLEN.

Warriors and Indian girls.

SCENE, *Virginia.*

THE INDIAN PRINCESS.

ACT I.

SCENE I.—*Powhatan River: wild and picturesque. Ships appear. Barges approach the shore, from which land* SMITH, ROLFE, PERCY, WALTER, LARRY, ROBIN, ALICE, &c.

CHORUS.

Jolly comrades, raise the glee,
Chorus it right cheerily ;
For the tempest's roar is heard no more,
And gaily we tread the wish'd-for shore :
    Then raise the glee merrily,
    Chorus it cheerily,
For past are the perils of the blust'ring sea.

Sm. ONCE more, my bold associates, welcome.
    Mark
What cheery aspects look upon our landing:
The face of Nature dimples o'er with smiles,
The heav'ns are cloudless, whiles the princely sun,
As glad to greet us in his fair domain,
Gives us gay salutation——
    Lar. (*to Walter*)   By St. Patrick
His fiery majesty does give warm welcome.
Arrah ! his gracious smiles are melting—

Wal.   Plague !
He burthens us with favours till we sweat.
    Sm. What think ye, Percy, Rolfe, have we not
        found
Sir Walter Raleigh faithful in his tale ?
Is't not a goodly land ? Along the bay,
How gay and lovely lie its skirting shores,
Fring'd with the summer's rich embroidery !
    Per. Believe me, sir, I ne'er beheld that spot
Where Nature holds more sweet varieties.
    Sm. The gale was kind that blew us hitherward.
This noble bay were undiscover'd still,
Had not that storm arose propitious,
And, like the ever kindly breath of heav'n,
Which sometimes rides upon the tempest's wing,
Driv'n us to happiest destinies, e'en then
When most we fear'd destruction from the blast.
    Rol. Let our dull sluggish countrymen at home
Still creep around their little isle of fogs,
Drink its dank vapours, and then hang themselves.
In this free atmosphere and ample range
The bosom can dilate, the pulses play,
And man, erect, can walk a manly round.
    Rob. (*aside*) Ay, and be scalp'd and roasted by
        the Indians.
    Sm. Now, gallant cavalier adventurers,
On this our landing spot we'll rear a town
Shall bear our good king's name to after-time,
And yours along with it ; for ye are men
Well worth the handing down ; whose paged names
Will not disgrace posterity to read :
Men born for acts of hardihood and valour,
Whose stirring spirits scorn'd to lie inert,

Base atoms in the mass of population
That rots in stagnant Europe. Ye are men
Who a high wealth and fame will bravely win,
And wear full worthily. I still shall be
The foremost in all troubles, toil, and danger,
Your leader and your captain, nought exacting
Save strict obedience to the watchful care
Which points to your own good: be wary then,
And let not any mutinous hand unravel
Our close knit compact. Union is its strength :
Be that remember'd ever. Gallant gentlemen,
We have a noble stage, on which to act
A noble drama ; let us then sustain
Our sev'ral parts with credit and with honour.
Now, sturdy comrades, cheerly to our tasks !
            [*Exeunt Smith, Rolfe, &c.*

SCENE II.—*A grove.*

Enter WALTER *and* LARRY.

Lar. Now by the black eyes of my Katy, but that master of yours and captain of mine is a prince !

Wal. Tut, you hav'n't seen an inch yet of the whole hero. Had you followed him as I have, from a knee-high urchin, you'd confess that there never was soldier fit to cry comrade to him. O ! 'twould have made your blood frisk in your veins to have seen him in Turkey and Tartary, when he made the clumsy infidels dance to the music of his broad sword !

Lar. Troth now, the mussulmans may have been mightily amused by the caper ; but for my part I should modestly prefer skipping to the simple jig of an Irish bag-pipe.

Wal. Then he had the prettiest mode of forming their manners——

Lar. Arrah, how might that be?

Wal. For example: whenever they were so ill-bred as to appear with their turbans on before him, he uses me this keen argument to convince them they showed discourtesy. He whips me out his sword, and knocks their turbans off——

Lar. Knocks their turbans off?

Wal. Ay, egad, and their heads to boot.

Lar. A dev'lish cutting way of reasoning indeed; that argument cou'dn't be answered asily.

Wal. Devil a tongue ever wagg'd in replication, Larry.—Ah! my fairy of felicity—my mouthful of melody—my wife——

Enter ALICE.

Well, Alice, we are now in the wilds of Virginia, and, tell me truly, doesn't repent following me over the ocean, wench? wilt be content in these wild woods, with only a little husband, and a great deal of love, pretty Alice?

Al. Can you ask that? are not all places alike if you are with me, Walter?

SONG.—*Alice.*

In this wild wood will I range;
    Listen, listen, dear!
Nor sigh for towns so fine, to change
    This forest drear.
Toils and dangers I'll despise,
    Never, never weary;
And be, while love is in thine eyes,
    Ever cheery.

Ah! what to me were cities gay;
    Listen, listen, dear!
If from me thou wert away,
    Alas! how drear!
O! still o'er sea, o'er land I'll rove,
    Never, never weary,
And follow on where leads my love,
    Ever cheery.

Lar. Och! the creature!

Wal. Let my lips tell thee what my tongue cannot.   [*kiss.*

Lar. Ay do, do stop her mellifluous mouth; for the little nightingale warbles so like my Kate, she makes me sigh for Ballinamone; ah! just so would the constant creature carol all day about, roving through the seas and over the woods.

Enter ROBIN.

Rob. Master Walter, the captain is a going to explore the country, and you must along.

Wal. That's our fine captain, always stirring.

Rob. Plague on his industry! would you think it, we are all incontinently to fall a chopping down trees, and building our own houses, like the beavers.

Lar. Well, sure, that's the fashionable mode of paying rent in this country.

Al. O, Walter, these merciless savages! I shan't be merry till you return——

Rob. I warrant ye, mistress Alice—Lord love you I shall be here.

Wal. Cheerly, girl; our captain will make the red rogues scamper like so many dun deer. Savages, quotha! at sight of him, their copper skins will

turn pale as silver, with the very alchemy of fear. Come, a few kisses, en passant, and then away! cheerly, my dainty Alice. [*Exeunt Walter and Alice.*

Rob. Ay, go your ways, master Walter, and when you are gone——

Lar. What then! I suppose you'll be after talking nonsense to his wife. But if ever I catch you saying your silly things——

Rob. Mum, Lord love you, how can you think it? But hark ye, master Larry, in this same drama that our captain spoke of, you and I act parts, do we not?

Lar. Arrah, to be sure, we are men of parts.

Rob. Shall I tell you in earnest what we play in this merry comedy?

Lar. Be doing it.

Rob. Then we play the parts of two fools, look you, to part with all at home, and come to these savage parts, where, Heaven shield us, our heads may be parted from our bodies. Think what a catastrophe, master Larry!

Lar. So the merry comedy ends a doleful tragedy, and exit fool in the character of a hero! That's glory, sirrah, a very feather in our cap.

Rob. A light gain to weigh against the heavy loss of one's head. Feather quotha! what use of a plumed hat without a head to wear it withal?

Lar. Tut man, our captain will lead us through all dangers.

Rob. Will he? an' he catch me following him through these same dangers——

Lar. Och, you spalpeen! I mean he'll lead us out of peril.

Rob. Thank him for nothing; for I've predetermined, look you, not to be led into peril. Oh, master Larry, what a plague had I to do to leave my snug cot and my brown lass, to follow master Rolfe to this devil of a country, where there's never a girl nor a house!

Lar. Out, you driveller! didn't I leave as neat a black-ey'd girl, and as pretty a prolific potatoe-patch all in tears——

Rob. Your potatoe-patch in tears! that's a bull, master Larry——

Lar. You're a calf, master Robin. Wasn't it raining? Och, I shall never forget it; the thunder rolling, and her tongue a going, and her tears and the rain; och bother, but it was a dismal morning!

SONG.—*Larry.*

I.

Och! dismal and dark was the day, to be sure,
When Larry took leave of sweet Katy Maclure;
And clouds dark as pitch hung just like a black lace
O'er the sweet face of Heav'n and my Katy's sweet face.
Then, while the wind blow'd, and she sigh'd might and main,
        Drops from the black skies
        Fell——and from her black eyes;
Och! how I was soak'd with her tears——and the rain.

(*Speaks*) And then she gave me this beautiful keep-sake (*shows a pair of scissors*), which if ever I part with, may a taylor clip me in two with his big shears. Och! when Katy took you in hand, how nicely did you snip and snap my bushy, carroty locks; and now you're cutting the hairs of my heart to pieces, you tieves you——

(*Sings*) Och! Hubbaboo—Gramachree—Hone!

II.

When I went in the garden, each bush seem'd to sigh
Becase I was going——and nod me good bye ;
Each stem hung its head, drooping bent like a bow,
With the weight of the water——or else of its woe ;
And while sorrow, or wind, laid some flat on the ground,
    Drops of rain, or of grief,
      Fell from every leaf,
Till I thought in a big show'r of tears I was drown'd.
(*Speaks*) And then each bush and leaf seem'd to sigh,
and say, " don't forget us, Larry." I won't, said I.——
" But arrah, take something for remembrance," said
they ; and then I dug up this neat jewel (*shows a potatoe*) ; you're a little withered to be sure, but if ever I forget your respectable family, or your delightful dwelling
place—may I never again see any of your beautiful brothers and plump sisters !—Och ! my darling, if you had
come hot from the hand of Katy, how my mouth would
have watered at ye ; now, you divil, you bring the water
into my eyes.
(*Sings*) Och ! Hubbaboo—Gramachree—Hone ! [*Exeunt.*

SCENE III.—*Werocomoco, the royal village of Powhatan. Indian girls arranging ornaments for a
bridal dress. Music.*

Nima. Let us make haste, my companions, to
finish the dress of the bride ; to-day the prince Miami returns with our hunters from the chase ; to-
morrow he will bear away our princess to his own
nation.

Enter POCAHONTAS *from the wood, with bow and
arrow, and a flamingo (red bird). Music as she
enters.*
Prs. See, Nima, a flamingo.

Indian girls crowd around, and admire the bird.
Prs. O Nima! I will use my bow no longer ; I
go out to the wood, and my heart is light ; but
while my arrow flies, I sorrow ; and when the bird
drops through the branches, tears come into mine
eyes. I will no longer use my bow.

*Distant hunting-horn. Music. They place them-
selves in attitudes of listening. Hunting-horn
nearer.*

Ni. 'Tis Miami and our hunters. Princess, why
are your looks sad ?
Prs. O Nima ! the prince comes to bear me far
from my father and my brother. I must quit for
ever the companions, and the woods that are dear to
me. Nima, the Susquehannocks are a powerful
nation, and my father would have them for his
friends. He gives his daughter to their prince, but
his daughter trembles to look upon the fierce Miami.

*Music. Hunters seen winding down the hills ; they
are met by the women of the village ;* MIAMI *ap-
proaches Pocahontas, and his attendants lay skins
at her feet.*

Mi. Princess, behold the spoils I bring thee.
Our hunters are laden with the deer and the soft
furred beaver. But Miami scorned such prey : I
watched for the mighty buffaloe and the shaggy
bear ; my club felled them to the ground, and I
tore their skins from their backs. The fierce carcajou had wound himself around the tree, ready to

dart upon the hunter ; but the hunter's eyes were
not closed, and the carcajou quivered on the point
of my spear. I heard the wolf howl as he looked at
the moon, and the beams that fell upon his upturned
face showed my tomahawk the spot it was to enter.
I marked where the panther had couched, and, before he could spring, my arrow went into his heart.
Behold the spoil the Susquehannock brings thee !
Pr. Susquehannock, thou'rt a mighty hunter.
Powhatan shall praise thee for his daughter. But
why returns not my brother with thee ?
Mi. Nantaquas still finds pleasure in the hunt, but
the soul of Miami grew weary of being away from
Werocomoco, for there dwelt the daughter of Pow-
hatan.
Pr. Let us go to my father.

*Music. Exeunt Princess and Miami into palace,
followed by Nima and train ; the others into their
several cabins.*

SCENE IV.—*A Forest.* SMITH *enters, bewildered in
its mazes. Music, expressive of his situation.*

Sm. 'Tis all in vain ! no clue to guide my steps.
                                       [*music.*
By this the explorers have return'd despairing,
And left their forward leader to his fate.
The rashness is well punish'd, that, alone,
Would brave the entangling mazes of these wilds.
The night comes on, and soon these gloomy woods
Will echo to the yell of savage beasts,
And savage men more merciless. Alas !
And am I, after all my golden dreams

Of laurel'd glory, doom'd in wilds to fall,
Ignobly and obscure, the prey of brutes ! [*music.*
Fie on these coward thoughts ! this trusty sword,
That made the Turk and Tartar crouch beneath me,
Will stead me well, e'en in this wilderness.
                                     [*music.*
O glory ! thou who led'st me fearless on,
Where death stalk'd grimly over slaughter'd heaps,
Or drank the drowning shrieks of shipwreck'd
    wretches,
Swell high the bosom of thy votary !
                         [*music. Exit Smith.*

Music. A party of Indians enter, as following
SMITH, *and steal cautiously after him. The Indian yell within. Music, hurried. Re-enter* SMITH,
*engaged with the Indians ; several fall. Exeunt,
fighting, and enter from the opposite side the Prince*
NANTAQUAS, *who views with wonder the prowess
of* SMITH *; when the music has ceased he speaks.*

Sure 'tis our war-god, Aresqui himself, who lays
our chiefs low ! Now they stop ; he fights no
longer ; he stands terrible as the panther, which the
fearful hunter dares not approach. Stranger, brave
stranger, Nantaquas must know thee ! [*music.*

He rushes out, and re-enters with SMITH.

Pr. Art thou not then a God ?
Sm. As thou art, warrior, but a man.
Pr. Then art thou a man like a God ; thou shalt
be the brother of Nantaquas. Stranger, my father

is king of the country, and many nations obey him: will thou be the friend of the great Powhatan?

Sm. Freely, prince; I left my own country to be the red man's friend.

Pr. Wonderful man, where is thy country?

Sm. It lies far beyond the wide water.

Pr. Is there then a world beyond the wide water? I thought only the sun had been there: thou comest then from behind the sun?

Sm. Not so, prince.

Pr. Listen to me. Thy country lies beyond the wide water, and from it do mine eyes behold the sun rise each morning.

Sm. Prince, to your sight he seems to rise from thence, but your eyes are deceived, they reach not over the wilderness of waters.

Pr. Where sleeps the sun then?

Sm. The sun never sleeps. When you see him sink behind the mountains, he goes to give light to other countries, where darkness flies before him, as it does here, when you behold him rise in the east: thus he chases Night for ever round the world.

Pr. Tell me, wise stranger, how came you from your country across the wide water? when our canoes venture but a little from the shore, the waves never fail to swallow them up.

Sm. Prince, the Great Spirit is the friend of the white men, and they have arts which the red men know not.

Pr. My brother, will you teach the red men?

Sm. I come to do it. My king is a king of a mighty nation; he is great and good: go, said he, go and make the red men wise and happy.

During the latter part of the dialogue, the Indians had crept in, still approaching till they had almost surrounded Smith. A burst of savage music. They seize and bear him off, the prince in vain endeavouring to prevent it.

Pr. Hold! the white man is the brother of your prince; hold, coward warriors!

[*he rushes out.*

SCENE V.—*Powhatan River, as the first scene.*

Enter LARRY.

Now do I begin to suspect, what, to be sure, I've been certain of a long time, that master Robin's a little bit of a big rogue. I just now observed him with my friend Walter's wife. Arrah! here they come. By your leave, fair dealing, I'll play the eavesdropper behind this tree.

[*retires behind a tree.*

Enter ALICE, *followed by* ROBIN.

Rob. But, mistress Alice, pretty Alice.

Al. Ugly Robin, I'll not hear a syllable.

Rob. But plague, prithee, Alice, why, so coy

Enter WALTER; *observing them, stops.*

Al. Master Robin, if you follow me about any longer with your fooleries, my Walter shall know of it.

Rob. A fig for Walter! is he to be mentioned the same day with the dapper Robin? can Walter make sonnets and madrigals, and set them, and sing them? besides, the Indians have eat him by this, I hope.

Wal. O the rascal!

Rob. Come, pretty one, quite alone, no one near, even that blundering Irishman away.

Lar. O you spalpeen! I'll blunder on you anon.

Rob. Shall we, Alice, shall we?

Quartetto.

Rob.	Mistress Alice, say,
	Walter's far away,
	Pretty Alice!
	Nay now—prithee, pray,
	Shall we, Alice? hey!
	Mistress Alice?
Al.	Master Robin, nay—
	Prithee go your way,
	Saucy Robin!
	If you longer stay,
	You may rue the day,
	Master Robin.
Wal. (aside)	True my Alice is.
Lar. (aside)	Wat shall know of this.
Rob. (struggling)	Pretty Alice!
Wal. (aside)	What a rascal 'tis!
Lar. (aside)	He'll kill poor Rob, I wis!
Rob. (struggling)	Mistress Alice,

	Let me taste the bliss—
	[*attempts to kiss her.*
Al.	Taste the bliss of this, [*slaps his face.*
	Saucy Robin!
Wal. (advancing)	O, what wond'rous bliss!
Lar. (advancing)	How d'ye like the kiss?
Al.	
Wal. }	Master Robin?
Lar.	

[*Robin steals off.*

Wal. Jackanapes!

Lar. Ay, hop off, cock robin! Blood and thunder now, that such a sparrow should try to turn hawk, and pounce on your little pullet here.

Al. Welcome, my bonny Walter.

Wal. A sweet kiss, Alice, to season my bitter tidings. Our captain's lost.

Har. } Lost!
Al.

Wal. You shall hear. A league or two below this, we entered a charming stream, that seemed to glide through a fairy land of fertility. I must know more of this, said our captain. Await my return here. So bidding us moor the pinnace in a broad bason, where the Indian's arrows could reach us from neither side, away he went, alone in his boat, to explore the river to its head.

Har. Gallant soul!

Wal. What devil prompted us to disobey his command I know not, but scarce was he out of sight, when we landed; and mark the end on't: up from their ambuscado started full three hundred black fiends, with a yell that might have appaled Lucifer, and whiz came a cloud of arrows about our ears.

Three tall fellows of ours fell ; Cassen, Emery, and Robinson. Our lieutenant, with Percy and myself, fought our way to the water side, where, leaving our canoe as a trophy to the victors, we plunged in, ducks, and, after swimming, dodging, and diving like regained the pinnace that we had left like geese.

Al. Heaven be praised, you are safe ; but our poor captain—

Wal. Ay ; the day passed and he returned not ; we came back for a reinforcement, and to-morrow we find him, or perish.

Al. Perish !—

Wal. Ay ; shame seize the poltroon who wou'dn't perish in such a cause ; wou'dn't you, Larry ?

Lar. By saint Patrick, it's the thing I would do, and 'hould my head the higher for it all the days of my life after.

Wal. But see, our lieutenant and master Percy.

Enter ROLFE *and* PERCY.

Rol. Good Walter look to the barge, see it be ready
By the earliest dawn.
Wal. I shall, sir.
Rol. And be careful,
This misadventure be not buzz'd abroad,
Where 't may breed mutiny and mischief. Say
We've left the captain waiting our return,
Safe with the other three ; meantime, chuse out
Some certain trusty fellows, who will swear
Bravely to find their captain or their death.
Wal. I'll hasten, sir, about it.

Lar. Good lieutenant,
Shall I along ?
Rol. In truth, brave Irishman,
We cannot have a better. Pretty Alice,
Will you again lose Walter for a time ?
Al. I would I were a man, sir, then, most willingly
I'd lose myself to do our captain service.
Rol. An Amazon !
Wal. O 'tis a valiant dove.
Lar. But come ; Heaven and St. Patrick prosper us.

[*Exeunt Walter, Larry, Alice.*

Rol. Now, my sad friend, cannot e'en this arouse you ?
Still bending with the weight of shoulder'd Cupid ?
Fie ! throw away that bauble, love, my friend :
That glist'ning toy of listless laziness,
Fit only for green girls and growing boys
T'amuse themselves withal. Can an inconstant,
A fickle changeling, move a man like Percy ?
Per. Cold youth ; how can you speak of that you feel not ?
You never lov'd.
Rol. Hum ! yes, in mine own way ;
Marry, 'twas not with sighs and folded arms ;
For mirth I sought in it, not misery.
Sir, I have ambled through all love's gradations
Most jollily, and seriously the whilst.
I have sworn oaths of love on my knee, yet laugh'd not ;
Complaints and chidings heard, but heeded not ;
Kiss'd the cheek clear from tear-drops, and yet wept not ;

Listen'd to vows of truth, which I believed not ;
And after have been jilted—
Per. Well !
Rol. And car'd not.
Per. Call you this loving ?
Rol. Ay, and wisely loving.
Not, sir, to have the current of one's blood
Froz'n with a frown, and molten with a smile ;
Make ebb and flood under a lady Luna,
Liker the moon in changing than in chasteness.
'Tis not to be a courier, posting up
To the seventh Heav'n, or down to the gloomy centre,
On the fool's errand of a wanton—pshaw !
Women ! they're made of whimsies and caprice,
So variant and so wild, that, ty'd to a God,
They'd dally with the devil for a change.—
Rather than wed a European dame,
I'd take a squaw o' the woods, and get papooses.
Per. If Cupid burn thee not for heresy,
Love is no longer catholic religion.
Rol. An' if he do, I'll die a sturdy martyr.
And to the last preach to thee, pagan Percy,
Till I have made a convert. Answer me,
Is not this idol of thy heathen worship
That sent thee hither a despairing pilgrim ;
Thy goddess, Geraldine, is she not false ?
Per. Most false !
Rol. For shame, then ; cease adoring her ;
Untwine the twisted cable of your arms,
Heave from your freighted bosom all its charge,
In one full sigh, and puff it strongly from you ;
Then, raising your earth-reading eyes to Heaven,

Laud your kind stars you were not married to her,
And so forget her.
Per. Ah ! my worthy Rolfe,
'Tis not the hand of infant Resolution
Can pluck this rooted passion from my heart :
Yet what I can I will ; by heaven ! I will.
Rol. Why, cheerly said ; the baby Resolution
Will grow apace ; time will work wonders in him.
Per. Did she not, after interchange of vows—
But let the false one go, I will forget her.
Your hand, my friend ; now will I act the man.
Rol. Faith, I have seen thee do't, and burn'd with shame,
That he who so could fight should ever sigh.
Per. Thinkst thou our captain lives ?
Rol. Tush ! he must live ;
He was not born to perish so. Believe't,
He'll hold these dingy devils at the bay,
Till we come up and succour him.
Per. And yet
A single arm against a host—alas !
I fear me he has fallen.
Rol. Then never fell
A nobler soul, more valiant, or more worthy,
Or fit to govern men. If he be gone,
Heaven save our tottering colony from falling !
But see, th' adventurers from their daily toil.

Enter adventurers, WALTER, LARRY, ROBIN, ALICE, &c.

Wal. Now, gentlemen labourers, a lusty roundelay after the toils of the day ; and then to a sound sleep, in houses of our own building.

Roundelay chorus.

Now crimson sinks the setting sun,
And our tasks are fairly done.
Jolly comrades, home to bed,
Taste the sweets by labour shed;
Let his poppy seal your eyes,
'Till another day arise,
For our tasks are fairly done,
As crimson sinks the setting sun.

ACT II.

SCENE I.—*Inside the palace at Werocomoco.* POW-
HATAN *in state,* GRIMOSCO, *&c., his wives, and
warriors, ranged on each side. Music.*

Pow. My people, strange beings have appeared among us; they come from the bosom of the
waters, amid fire and thunder; one of them has
our war-god delivered into our hands: behold the
white being!

Music. SMITH *is brought in; his appearance excites
universal wonder;* POCAHONTAS *expresess peculiar admiration.*

Poc. O Nima! is it not a God!
Pow. Miami, though thy years are few, thou
art experienced as age; give us thy voice of counsel.
Mia. Brothers, this stranger is of a fearful
race of beings; their barren hunting grounds lie

beneath the world, and they have risen, in mon-
strous canoes, through the great water, to spoil
and ravish from us our fruitful inheritance. Brothers, this stranger must die; six of our brethren
have fall'n by his hand. Before we lay their bones
in the narrow house, we must avenge them: their
unappeased spirits will not go to rest beyond the
mountains; they cry out for the stranger's blood.
Nan. Warriors, listen to my words; listen, my
father, while your son tells the deeds of the brave
white man. I saw him when 300 of our fiercest
chiefs formed the war-ring around him. But he
defied their arms; he held lightning in his hand.
Wherever his arm fell, there sunk a warrior: as the
tall tree falls, blasted and riven, to the earth, when
the angry Spirit darts his fires through the forest.
I thought him a god; my feet grew to the ground;
I could not move!
Poc. Nima, dost thou hear the words of my
brother?
Nan. The battle ceased, for courage left the bosom of our warriors; their arrows rested in their
quivers; their bowstrings no longer sounded; the
tired chieftains leaned on their war-clubs, and gazed
at the terrible stranger, whom they dared not approach. Give an ear to me, king: 'twas then I
held out the hand of peace to him, and he became
my brother; he forgot his arms, for he trusted to
his brother; he was discoursing wonders to his
friend, when our chiefs rushed upon him, and
bore him away. But oh! my father, he must not
die; for he is not a war captive; I promised that
the chain of friendship should be bright between us.

Chieftains, your prince must not falsify his word;
father, your son must not be a liar!
Poc. Listen, warriors; listen, father; the white man
is my brother's brother!
Grim. King! when last night our village shook
with the loud noise, it was the Great Spirit who
talk'd to his priest; my mouth shall speak his
commands: King, we must destroy the strangers,
for they are not our God's children; we must take
their scalps, and wash our hands in the white man's
blood, for he is an enemy to the Great Spirit.
Nan. O priest, thou hast dreamed a false dream;
Miami, thou tellest the tale that is not. Hearken,
my father to my true words! the white man is beloved by the Great Spirit; his king is like you, my
father, good and great; and he comes from a land
beyond the wide water, to make us wise and happy!

Powhatan deliberates. Music.

Pow. Stranger, thou must prepare for death.
Six of our brethren fell by thy hand. Thou must
die.
Poc. Father, O father!
Sm. Had not your people first beset me, king,
I would have prov'd a friend and brother to them;
Arts I'd have taught, that should have made them
        gods,
And gifts would I have given to your people,
Richer than red men ever yet beheld.
Think not I fear to die. Lead to the block.
The soul of the white warrior shall shrink not.
Prepare the stake! amidst your fiercest tortures,
You'll find its fiery pains as nobly scorned,
As when the red man sings aloud his death-song.

Poc. Oh! shall that brave man die!

*Music. The king motions with his hand, and
Smith is led to the block.*

Mi. (*to executioners*) Warriors, when the third
signal strikes, sink your tomahawks in his head.
Poc. Oh, do not, warriors, do not! Father, incline
your heart to mercy; he will win your battles, he
will vanquish your enemies. (*1st signal*) Brother,
speak! save your brother! Warriors, are you brave?
preserve the brave man! (*2d signal*) Miami, priest,
sing the song of peace; ah! strike not, hold!
mercy!

*Music. The 3d signal is struck, the hatchets are
lifted up: when the princess, shrieking, runs
distractedly to the block, and presses Smith's head
to her bosom.*

White man, thou shalt not die; or I will die with
thee!

Music. She leads Smith to the throne, and kneels.

My father, dost thou love thy daughter? listen to
her voice; look upon her tears: they ask for mercy
to the captive. Is thy child dear to thee, my father?
Thy child will die with the white man.

*Plaintive music. She bows her head to his feet. Pow-
hatan, after some deliberation, looking on his daughter with tenderness, presents her with a string of
white wampum. Pocahontas, with the wildest ex-
pression of joy, rushes forward with Smith, pre-
senting the beads of peace.*

Captive ! thou art free !—

Music. General joy is diffused—Miami and Grimosco only appear discontented. The prince Nantaquas congratulates Smith. The princess shows the most extravagant emotions of rapture.

Sm. O woman ! angel sex ! where'er thou art,
Still art thou heavenly. The rudest clime
Robs not thy glowing bosom of it's nature.
Thrice blessed lady, take a captive's thanks !
                    [*he bows upon her hand.*
Poc. My brother !—
          [*music. Smith expresses his gratitude.*
Nan. Father, hear the design that fills my breast.
I will go among the white men ; I will learn their
arts ; and my people shall be made wise and happy.
Poc. I too will accompany my brother.
Mi. Princess !—
Poc. Away, cruel Miami ; you would have murdered my brother !—
Poc. Go, my son ; take thy warriors, and go with
the white men. Daughter, I cannot lose thee from
mine eyes ; accompany thy brother but a little on
his way. Stranger, depart in peace ; I entrust my
son to thy friendship.
Sm. Gracious sir,
He shall return with honours and with wonders ;
My beauteous sister ! noble brother come !

Music. Exeunt, on one side, Smith, princess, Nantaquas, Nima, and train. On the other, king, priest, Miami, &c. The two latter express angry discontent.

SCENE II.—*A forest.*

Enter PERCY, ROLFE.

Rol. So far indeed 'tis fruitless, yet we'll on.
Per. Ay, to the death.
Rol.   Brave Percy, come, confess
You have forgot your love.
Per.   Why faith, not quite ;
Despite of me, it sometimes through my mind
Flits like a dark cloud o'er a summer sky ;
But passes off like that, and leaves me cloudless.
I can't forget that she was sweet as spring ;
Fair as the day.
Rol.   Ay, ay, like April weather ;
Sweet, fair, and faithless.
Per.   True, alas ! like April !

SONG—*Percy.*

Fair Geraldine each charm of spring possest,
     Her cheek glow'd with the rose and lily's strife ;
Her breath was perfume, and each winter'd breast
     Felt that her sunny eyes beam'd light and life.

Alas ! that in a form of blooming May,
     The mind should April's changeful liv'ry wear !
Yet ah ! like April, smiling to betray,
     Is Geraldine, as false as she is fair !

Rol. Beshrew the little gipsey ! let us on.
                    [*Exeunt Percy, Rolfe.*

Enter LARRY, WALTER, ROBIN, &c.

Lar. Go no further ? Och ! you hen-hearted cock
robin !

Rob. But, master Larry—
Wal. Prithee, thou evergreen aspen leaf, thou
non-intermittent ague ! why didst along with us ?
Rob. Why, you know, my master Rolfe desired it ;
and then you were always railing out on me for
chicken-heartedness. I came to show ye I had valour.
Wal. But forgetting to bring it with thee, thou
wouldst now back for it ; well, in the name of Mars,
go ; return for thy valour, Robin.
Rob. What ! alone ?
Lar. Arrah ! then stay here till it come to you,
and then follow us.
Rob. Stay here ! O Lord, methinks I feel an arrow sticking in my gizzard already ! Harkye, my
sweet master, let us sing.
Lar. Sing ?
Rob. Sing ; I'm always valiant when I sing. Beseech you, let us chaunt the glee that I dish'd up
for us three.
Lar. It has a spice of your cowardly cookery in it.
Wal. But since 'tis a provocative to Robin's valour—
Lar. Go to : give a lusty hem, and fall on.

Glee.

We three, adventurers be,
Just come from our own country ;
We have cross'd thrice a thousand ma,
Without a penny of money.

We three, good fellows be,
Who wou'd run like the devil from Indians three ;
We never admir'd their bowmandry ;
O give us whole skins for our money.

We three, merry men be,
Who gaily will chaunt our ancient glee,
Though a lass or a glass, in this wild country,
Can't be had, or for love, or for money.

Lar. Well, how do you feel ?
Rob. As courageous as, as a——
Lar. As a wren, little Robin. Are you sure, now,
you won't be after fancying every deer that skips
by you a devil, and every bush a bear ?
Rob. I defy the devil ; but havn't you heard, my
masters, how the savages go a hunting, drest out
in deer-skin ? How could you put one in mind, master Larry ? O Lord ! that I should come a captain-
hunting ! the only game we put up is deer that
carry scalping knives ! or if we beat the bush to
start a bold commander, up bolts a bloody bear !
          [*Walter and Larry exchange significant nods.*
Lar. To be sure we're in a parlous case. The
forest laws are dev'lish severe here : an they catch
us trespassing upon their hunting ground, we
shall pay a neat poll-tax : nothing less than our
heads will serve.
Rob. Our heads ?
Wal. Yes, faith ! they'll soon collect their capitation.
They wear men's heads, sir, hanging at the breast,
Instead of jewels ; and at either ear,
Most commonly, a child's, by way of ear-drop.
Rob. O ! curse their finery ! jewels, heads, O
     Lord !
Lar. Pshaw, man ! don't fear. Perhaps they'll
     only burn us.
What a delicate roasted Robin you wou'd make !

Troth! they'd so lick their lips!

Rob.   A roasted robin!——

Wal. Tut! if they only burn us, 'twill be brave.
Robin shall make our death-songs.

Rob.   Death-songs, oh!

[*Robin stands motionless with fear.*

Lar. By the good looking right eye of Saint Patrick,
There's Rolfe and Percy, with a tribe of Indians,

[*looking out.*

Rob. Indians! they're pris'ners, and we—we're dead men!

While Walter and Larry exeunt, Robin gets up into a tree.

O Walter, Larry! ha! what gone, all gone!
Poor Robin, what is to become of thee?

Enter SMITH, POCAHONTAS, NANTAQUAS, PERCY, ROLFE, NIMA *and Indians*, LARRY, *and* WALTER.

Sm. At hazard of her own dear life she saved me.
E'en the warm friendship of the prince had fail'd,
And death, inevitable death, hung over me.
O had you seen her fly, like Pity's herald,
To stay the uplifted hatchet in its flight;
Or heard her, as with cherub voice she pled,
Like Heav'n's own angel-advocate, for mercy.

Poc. My brother, speak not so.   [*bashfully.*

Rol.   What gentleness!
What sweet simplicity! what angel softness!

Rolfe goes to her. She, timidly, but with evident pleasure, receives his attentions. During this scene the

princess discovers the first advances of love in a heart of perfect simplicity. Smith, &c., converse apart.

Rob. (in the tree) Egad! there's never a head hanging to their ears; and their ears hang to their heads, for all the world as if they were christians; I'll venture down among them.   [*getting down.*

Ni. Ah!

[*bends her bow, and is about to shoot at him.*

Lar. Arrah! my little dark Diana, choose noble game, that's only little Robin.

Rob. Ay, bless you, I'm only little Robin.

[*jumps down.*

Nima examines him curiously, but fearfully.

Rob. Gad, she's taken with my figure; ah! there it is now; a personable fellow shall have his wench any where. Yes, she's admiring my figure. Well, my dusky dear, how could you like such a man as I am?

Ni. Are you a man?

Rob. I'll convince you of it some day. Hark ye, my dear.   [*attempts to whisper.*

Ni. Ah! don't bite.

Rob. Bite! what do you take me for?

Ni. A racoon.

Rob. A racoon! Why so?

Ni. You run up the tree. [*motions as if climbing.*

Lar. Well said, my little pagan Pythagoras!—ha! ha!

Rob. Hum!   [*retires disconcerted.*

Rolfe and Percy come forward.

Rol. Tell me, in sooth, didst ever mark such sweetness!
Such winning—such bewitching gentleness!

Per. What, caught, my flighty friend, love-lim'd at last?
O Cupid, Cupid! thou'rt a skilful birder.
Although thou spread thy net, i' the wilderness,
Or shoot thy bird-bolt from an Indian bow,
Or place thy light in savage ladies' eyes,
Or pipe thy call in savage ladies' voices,
Alas! each tow'ring tenant of the air
Must fall heart pierc'd—or stoop, at thy command,
To sigh his sad notes in thy cage, O Cupid!

Rol. A truce; a truce! O, friend, her guiltless breast
Seems Love's pavilion, where, in gentle sleep,
The unrous'd boy has rested. O, my Percy!
Could I but wake the slumb'rer——

Per.   Nay, i' faith,
Take courage; thou hast given the alarm:
Methinks the drowsy god gets up apace.

Rol. Say'st thou?

Sm.   Come, gentlemen, we'll toward the town.

Nan. My sister, you will now return to our father.

Prs. Return, my brother?

Nan. Our father lives but while you are near him.
Go, my sister, make him happy with the knowledge of his son's happiness. Farewell, my sister!

[*the princess appears dejected.*

Sm. Once more, my guardian angel, let me thank thee.   [*kissing her hand.*

Ere long we will return to thee, with presents
Well worth a princess' and a king's acceptance.
Meantime, dear lady, tell the good Powhatan
We'll show the prince such grace and entertainment,
As shall befit our brother and his son.
Adieu, sweet sister.

Music.   They take leave of the princess; she remains silently dejected; her eyes anxiously follow Rolfe, who lingers behind, and is the last to take leave.

Prs. Stranger, wilt thou too come to Werocomoco?

Rol. Dost thou wish it, lady?

Prs. (eagerly) O yes!

Rol. And why, lovely lady?

Prs. My eyes are pleased to see thee, and my ears to hear thee, stranger.

Rol. And did not the others who were here also please thy sight and hearing?

Prs. O! they were all goodly; but—their eyes looked not like thine; their voices sounded not like thine; and their speeches were not like thy speeches, stranger.

Rol. Enchanting simplicity! But why call me stranger? Captain Smith thou callest brother. Call me so too.

Prs. Ah, no!

Rol. Then thou thinkest not of me as thou dost of him? *(she shakes her head and sighs)* Is captain Smith dear to thee?

Prs. O yes! very dear; *(Rolfe is uneasy)* and Nantaquas too: they are my brothers;—but—that name is not thine—thou art——

Rol. What, lovely lady?

Prs. I know not; I feel the name thou art, but I cannot speak it.

Rol. I am thy lover, dear princess.

Prs. Yes, thou art my lover.   But why call me princess?

Rol. Dear lady, thou art a king's daughter.

Prs. And if I were not, what would'st thou call me?

Rol. Oh! if thou wert a beggar's, I would call thee love!

Prs. I know not what a beggar is; but oh! I would I were a beggar's daughter, so thou wouldst call me love. Ah! do not any longer call me king's daughter. If thou feelest the name as I do, call me as I call thee: thou shalt be *my* lover; I will be *thy* lover.

Rol. Enchanting, lovely creature!

[*Kisses her ardently.*

Prs. Lover, thou hast made my cheek to burn, and my heart to beat! Mark it.

Rol. Dear innocence!

[*Putting his hand to her heart.*

Prs. Lover, why is it so? To day before my heart beat, and mine eyes were full of tears; but then my white brother was in danger. Thou art not in danger, and yet behold—(*Wipes a tear from her eye.*) Besides, then, my heart hurt me, but now! O now!—Lover why is it so?

[*Leaning on him with innocent confidence.*

Rol. Angel of purity! thou didst to day feel pity;

and now—O rapturous task to teach thee the difference!—now, thou dost feel love.

Prs. Love!

Rol. Love: the noblest, the sweetest passion that could swell thy angel bosom.

Prs. O! I feel that 'tis very sweet. Lover, with thy lips thou didst make me feel it. My lips shall teach thee sweet love. (*Kisses him, and artlessly looks up in his face; placing her hand upon his heart.*) Does thy heart beat?

Rol. Beat! O heaven!—

[*Robin, who had been with Nima, comes forward.*

Rob. Gad! we must end our amours, or we shall be left. Sir, my master, hadn't we better—

Rol. Booby! ideot!

Enter WALTER.

Wal. Sir, lieutenant, the captain awaits your coming up.

Rol. I'll follow on the instant.

Prs. Thou wilt not go?

Rol. But for a time, love.

Prs. I do not wish thee to leave me.

Rol. I must, love; but I will return.

Prs. Soon—very soon?

Rol. Very—very soon.

Prs. I am not pleased now—and yet my heart beats. Oh, lover!

Rol. My angel! there shall not a sun rise and set, ere I am with thee. Adieu! thy own heavenly innocence be thy safeguard. Farewell, sweet love!

Music. He embraces her and exit, followed by Robin and Walter. Princess looks after him. A pause.

Prs. O Nima!

Ni. Princess, white men are pow-wows. The white man put his lips here, and I felt something— here—   [*putting her hand to her heart.*

Prs. O lover!

She runs to the place whence Rolfe went out, and gazes after him. Music. Enter from opposite side, MIAMI.

Mi. (*sternly*) Princess!

Prs. (*turning*) Ah!

Mi. Miami has followed thy steps. Thou art the friend of the white men.

Prs. Yes, for they are good and godlike.

Mi. Mine eyes beheld the pale youth part from you; your arms were entwined, your lips were together!   [*struggling with jealousy.*

Prs. He is my lover; I am his lover.

[*still looking after Rolfe.*

Mi. (*stamps with anger*) Hear me! In what do the red yield to the white men? and who among the red men is like Miami? While I was yet a child, did the dart which my breath blew through my sarbacan ever fail to pierce the eye of the bird? What youth dared, like Miami, to leap from the precipice, and drag the struggling bear from the foaming torrent? Is there a hunter—is there a warrior—skilful and brave as Miami? Come to my cabin, and see the scalps and the skins that adorn it. They are the trophies of the Susquehannock!

Prs. Man, mine eyes will never behold thy trophies. They are not pleased to look on thee.

[*averting her eyes with disgust.*

Mi. Ha! (*pause—he resumes in a softened tone.*) Princess, I have crossed many woods and waters, that I might bear the daughter of Powhatan to my nation. Shall my people cry out, with scorn, "behold! our prince returns without his bride!" In what is the pale youth above the red Miami?

Prs. Thine eyes are as the panther's; thy voice like the voice of the wolf. Thou shouldst make my heart beat with joy; and I tremble before thee. O no! Powhatan shall give me to my lover. I will be my lover's bride!

Music. Miami stamps furiously; his actions betray the most savage rage of jealousy; he rushes to seize the princess, but, recollecting that her attendants are by, he goes out in an agony, by his gestures menacing revenge. The princess exit on the opposite side, followed by train.

SCENE III.—*Werocomoco.*

Music. Enter from the palace POWHATAN *and* GRIMOSCO; *met by the* PRINCESS, *who runs to her father.*

Pow. My daughter!

Prs. O father! the furious Miami!

Pow. What of the prince?

Prs. Father, my father! do not let the fierce prince bear me to his cruel nation!

Pow. How!

Prs. By the spirit of my mother, I implore my father. Oh! if thou deliver me to the Susquehannock, think not thine eyes shall ever again behold me; the first kind stream that crosses our path shall be the end of my journey; my soul shall seek the soul of the mother that loved me, far beyond the mountains.

Pow. Daughter, mention not thy mother!

Prs. Her shade will pity her unhappy child, and I shall be at rest in her bosom.   [*weeping.*

Pow. Rest in my bosom, my child! (*she starts with joyful emotion.*) Thou shalt not go from thy father.

Prs. Father; dear father!   [*seizing his hand.*

Music. An Indian enters, bearing a red hatchet.

In. King!

Pow. Thou art of the train of the Susquehannock: speak.

In. My prince demands his bride.
          [*the princess clings fearfully to the king.*

Pow. Tell thy prince, my daughter will not leave her father.

In. Will Powhatan forget his promise to Miami?

Pow. Powhatan will not forget his promise to her mother; and he vowed, while the angel of death hovered over her, that the eye of tender care should never be averted from her darling daughter.

In. Shall not then my prince receive his bride?

Pow. The daughter of Powhatan—never.

In. Take then his defiance.
          [*music. He presents the red hatchet.*

Pow. The red hatchet! 'Tis well. Grimosco, summon our warriors.

Gri. O king! might I—

Pow. Speak not. Tell our chiefs to assemble; and show them the war-signal. (*Exit Grimosco*) Go, tell your master, the great Powhatan will soon meet him, terrible as the minister of vengeance. (*exit Indian.*) The chiefs approach. My child, retire from this war scene.

Prs. O dear parent! thine age should have been passed in the shade of peace; and do I bring my father to the bloody war-path?

Pow. Not so; the young prince has often dared my power, and merited my vengeance; he shall now feel both.

Prs. Alas! his nation is numerous and warlike

Pow. Fear not, my child; we will call the valiant Nantaquas from his brothers; the brave English too will join us.

Prs. Ah! then is thy safety and success certain,
          [*exit into palace, followed by Nima, &c.*

Music. Enter Grimosco *and Warriors.*

Pow. Brave chieftains! need I remind you of the victories you have gained; the scalps you have borne from your enemies? Chieftains, another victory must be won; more trophies from your foes must deck your cabins; the insolent Miami has braved your king, and defied him with the crimson tomahawk. Warriors! we will not bury it till his nation is extinct. Ere we tread the war-path, raise

to our god Aresqui the song of battle, then march to triumph and to glory.

Song to Aresqui.

Aresqui! Aresqui!
Lo! thy sons for war prepare!
  Snakes adorn each painted head,
  While the cheek of flaming red
Gives the eye its ghastly glare.
  Aresqui! Aresqui!
Through the war-path lead aright,
Lo! we're ready for the fight.

War Song.

First Ind.   See the cautious warrior creeping!
Second Ind. See the tree-hid warrior peeping!
First Ind.   Mark! Mark!
  Their track is here; now breathless go!
Second Ind.   Hark! Hark!
  The branches rustle—'tis the foe!
Chorus.   Now we bid the arrow fly—
  Now we raise the hatchet high.
  Where is urg'd the deadly dart,
  There is pierced a chieftain's heart;
  Where the war-club swift descends,
  A hero's race of glory ends!
First Ind.   In vain the warrior flies—
  From his brow the scalp we tear.
Second Ind. Or home the captiv'd prize,
  A stake-devoted victim, bear.
First & Sec. Ind.   The victors advance—
  And while amidst the curling blaze,
  Our foe his death-song tries to raise—
  Dance the warriors' dance.
          [*War-dance.*
Grand Chorus.   Aresqui! Aresqui!
  Through the war-path lead aright—
  Lo! we're ready for the fight.
          [*March to battle.*

ACT III.

Scene 1.—*Jamestown—built.*

Walter *and* Alice.

Wal. One mouthful more (*kiss*). Oh! after a long lent of absence, what a charming relish is a kiss, served from the lips of a pretty wife, to a hungry husband.

Al. And, believe me, I banquet at the high festival of return with equal pleasure. But what has made your absence so tedious, prithee?

Wal. Marry, girl, thus it was: when we had given the enemies of our ally, Powhatan, defeature, and sent the rough Miami in chains to Werocomoco, our captain dispatches his lieutenant, Rolfe, to supply his place, here, in the town; and leading us to the water's edge, and leaping into the pinnace, away went we on a voyage of discovery. Some thousand miles we sailed, and many strange nations discovered; and for our exploits, if posterity reward us not, there is no faith in history.

Al. And what were your exploits?

Wal.   Rare ones egad!
We took the devil, Okee, prisoner.

Al. And have you brought him hither?

Wal.   No: his vot'ries
Redeem'd him with some score or two of deer-skins.
Then we've made thirty kings our tributaries:

Such sturdy rogues, that each could easily
Fillip a buffaloe to death with 's finger.
 Al. But have you got their treasures?
 Wal.   All, my girl.
Imperial robes of raccoon, crowns of feather;
Besides the riches of their sev'ral kingdoms——
A full boat load of corn.
 Al.   O wonderful!
 Wal. Ay, is it not?   But, best of all, I've kiss'd
The little finger of a mighty queen.
Sweet soul! among the court'sies of her court,
She gave us a Virginian mascarado.
 Al. Dost recollect the fashion of it?
 Wal.   Oh!
Were I to live till Time were in his dotage,
'Twould never from mine eyes.   Imagine first,
The scene, a gloomy wood; the time, midnight;
Her squawship's maids of honour were the mas-
    quers;
Their masks were wolves' heads curiously set on,
And, bating a small difference of hue,
Their dress e'en such as madam Eve had on
Or ere she eat the apple.
 Al.   Pshaw!
 Wal.   These dresses,
All o'er perfum'd with the self-same pomado
Which our fine dames at home buy of old Bruin,
Glisten'd most gorgeously unto the moon.
Thus, each a firebrand brandishing aloft,
Rush'd they all forth, with shouts and frantic yells,
In dance grotesque and diabolical,
Madder than mad Bacchantes.
 Al.   O the powers!

 Wal. When they had finished the divertisement
A beauteous Wolf-head came to me—
 Al.   To you?
 Wal. And lit me with her pine-knot torch to bed-
    ward,
Where, as the custom of the court it was,
The beauteous Wolf-head blew the flambeau out,
And then—
 Al.   Well!
 Wal.   Then, the light being out, you know,
To all that follow'd I was in the dark.
Now you look grave.   In faith I went to sleep.
Could a grim wolf rival my gentle lamb?
No, truly, girl: though in this wilderness
The trees hang full of divers colour'd fruit,
From orange-tawny to sloe-black, egad,
They'll hang until they rot or ere I pluck them,
While I've my melting, rosy nonpareil. [*kiss.*
 Al. O! you're a Judas!
 Wal.   Then am I a Jew!

Enter SMITH, PERCY, NANTAQUAS, LARRY, &c.

 Sm. Yet, prince, accept at least my ardent
    thanks:
A thousand times told over, they would fail
To pay what you and your dear sister claim.
Through my long absence from my people here,
You have sustain'd their feebleness.
 Nan.   O, brother,
To you, the conqueror of our father's foes;
To you, the sun which from our darken'd minds
Has chas'd the clouds of error, what can we

Not to remain your debtors?
 Sm.   Gen'rous soul!
Your friendship is my pride.   But who knows
    aught
Of our young Rolfe?
 Per.   This morning, sir, I hear,
An hour ere our arrival, the lieutenant
Accompanied the princess to her father's.
 Sm. Methinks our laughing friend has found at
    last
The power of sparkling eyes.   What say you,
    prince,
To a brave, worthy soldier for your brother?
 Nan. Were I to chuse, I'd put all others by
To make his path-way clear unto my sister.
But come, sir, shall we to my father's banquet?
One of my train I've sent to give him tidings
Of your long-wish'd for coming.
 Sm.   Gentle prince,
You greet my fresh return with welcome summons,
And I obey it cheerfully.   Good Walter,
And, worthy sir *(to Larry)*, be it your care
To play the queen bee here, and keep the swarm
Still gathering busily.   Look to it well:
Our new-raised hive must hold no drones within it.
Now, forward, sirs, to Werocomoco.
    [*exeunt Smith, Prince, Percy, &c.*

Manent Walter and Larry.

 Wal. So, my compeer in honour, we must hold
The staff of sway between us.

 Lar.   Arrah, man,
If we hould it between us, any rogue
Shall run clean off before it knocks him down,
While at each end we tug for mastery.
 Wal. Tush man! we'll strike in unison.
 Lar.   Go to—
 Wal. And first, let's to the forest—the young
    sparks
In silken doublets there are felling trees,
Poor gentle masters, with their soft palms blister'd;
And, while they chop and chop, they swear and
    swear,
Drowning with oaths the echo of their axe.
 Lar. Are they so hot in choler?
 Wal.   Ay.
 Lar.   We'll cool 'em;
And pour cold patience down their silken sleeves.
 Wal. Cold patience!
 Lar.   In the shape of water, honey.
 Wal. A notable discovery; come away!
 Lar. Ha! isn't that a sail?
 Wal.   A sail! a fleet!
    [*looking toward the river.*

Enter TALMAN.

 Tal. We have discovered nine tall ships.
 Lar.   Discovered!
Away, you rogue, we have discovered them,
With natures telescopes.   Run—scud—begone—
Down to the river!   Och, St. Pat, I thank you!
*Go toward the river.   Huzza within.   Music ex-
presses joyful bustle.   Scene closes.*

SCENE II.—*A grove.*

Enter ROBIN *and* NIMA.

Rob. Ay, bless you, I knew I should creep into your heart at last, my little dusky divinity.

Ni. Divinity! what's that?

Rob. Divinity—it's a—O it's a pretty title that we lords of the creation bestow upon our play-things. But hist! here they come. Now is it a knotty point to be argued, whether this parting doth most affect the mistress and master, or the maid and man. Let Cupid be umpire, and steal the scales of Justice to weigh our heavy sighs.
[*retire.*

Enter ROLFE *and* POCAHONTAS.

Prs. Nay, let me on——

Rol. No further, gentle love;
The rugged way has wearied you already.

Prs. Feels the wood pigeon weariness, who flies,
Mated with her beloved? Ah! lover, no.

Rol. Sweet! in this grove we will exchange adieus;
My steps should point straight onward; were thou with me,
Thy voice would bid me quit the forward path
At every pace, or fix my side-long look,
Spell-bound, upon thy beauties.

Prs. Ah! you love not
The wild-wood prattle of the Indian maid.

As once you did.

Rol. By heaven! my thirsty ear,
Could ever drink its liquid melody.
Oh! I could talk with thee, till hasty night,
Ere yet the centinel day had done his watch;
Veil'd like a spy, should steal on printless feet,
To listen to our parley! Dearest love!
My captain has arrived, and I do know,
When honour and when duty call upon me,
Thou wouldst not have me chid for tardiness.
But, ere the matin of to-morrow's lark,
Do echo from the roof of nature's temple,
Sweetest, expect me.

Prs. Wilt thou surely come?

Rol. To win thee from thy father will I come;
And my commander's voice shall join with mine,
To woo Powhatan to resign his treasure.

Prs. Go then, but ah! forget not——

Rol. I'll forget
All else, to think on thee!

Prs. Thou art my life!
I lived not till I saw thee, love; and now,
I live not in thine absence. Long, O! long
I was the savage child of savage Nature;
And when her flowers sprang up, while each green bough
Sang with the passing west wind's rustling breath;
When her warm visitor, flush'd Summer, came,
Or Autumn strew'd her yellow leaves around,
Or the shrill north wind pip'd his mournful music,
I saw the changing brow of my wild mother
With neither love nor dread. But now, O! now,
I could entreat her for eternal smiles,

So thou might'st range through groves of loveliest flowers,
Where never Winter, with his icy lip,
Should dare to press thy cheek.

Rol. My sweet enthusiast!

Prs. O! 'tis from thee that I have drawn my being:
Thou'st ta'en me from the path of savage error,
Blood-stain'd and rude, where rove my countrymen,
And taught me heavenly truths, and fill'd my heart
With sentiments sublime, and sweet, and social.
Oft has my winged spirit, following thine,
Cours'd the bright day-beam, and the star of night,
And every rolling planet of the sky,
Around their circling orbits. O, my love!
Guided by thee, has not my daring soul,
O'ertopt the far off mountains of the east,
Where, as our fathers fable, shad'wy hunters
Pursue the deer, or clasp the melting maid,
Mid ever blooming spring? Thence, soaring high
From the deep vale of legendary fiction,
Hast thou not heaven-ward turn'd my dazzled sight,
Where sing the spirits of the blessed good
Around the bright throne of the Holy One?
This thou hast done; and ah! what couldst thou more,
Belov'd preceptor, but direct that ray,
Which beams from heaven to animate existence,
And bid my swelling bosom beat with love!

Rol. O, my dear scholar!

Prs. Prithee chide me, love:
My idle prattle holds thee from thy purpose.

Rol. O! speak more music! and I'll listen to it,
Like stilly midnight to sweet Philomel.

Prs. Nay, now begone; for thou must go: ah! fly,
The sooner to return——

Rol. Thus, then, adieu! [*embrace.*
But, ere the face of morn blush rosy red,
To see the dew-besprent, cold virgin ground
Stain'd by licentious step; O, long before
The foot of th' earliest furred forrester,
Do mark its imprint on morn's misty sheet,
With sweet good morrow will I wake my love.

Prs. To bliss thou'lt wake me, for I sleep till then
Only with sorrow's poppy on my lids.

Music. Embrace; and exit Rolfe, followed by Robin; Princess looks around despondingly.

But now, how gay and beauteous was this grove!
Sure ev'ning's shadows have enshrouded it,
And 'tis the screaming bird of night I hear,
Not the melodious mock-bird. Ah! fond girl!
'Tis o'er thy soul the gloomy curtain hangs;
'Tis in thy heart the rough-toned raven sings.
O, lover! haste to my benighted breast;
Come like the glorious sun, and bring me day!

SONG.

When the midnight of absence the day-scene pervading
    Distils its chill dew o'er the bosom of love,
O how fast then the gay tints of nature are fading!
    How harsh seems the music of joy in the grove!
While the tender flow'r droops till return of the light,
Steep'd in tear drops that fall from the eye of the night.

But O, when the lov'd-one appears,
  Like the sun a bright day to impart,
To kiss off those envious tears,
  To give a new warmth to the heart ;
    Soon the flow'ret seeming dead
    Raises up its blushing head,
    Glows again the breast of love,
    Laughs again the joyful grove ;
    While once more the mock-bird's throat
    Trolls the sweetly various note.
But ah ! when dark absence the day-scene pervading
  Distils its chill dew o'er the bosom of love,
O ! fast then the gay tints of nature are fading !
O ! harsh seems the music of joy in the grove !
And the tender flow'r droops till return of the light,
Steep'd in tear drops that fall from the eye of the night.

Prs. Look, Nima, surely I behold our captive,
The prince Miami, and our cruel priest.
Ni. Lady, 'tis they ; and now they move this way.
Prs. How earnest are their gestures ; ah ! my
    Nima,
When souls like theirs mingle in secret council,
Stern murder's voice alone is listen'd to.
Miami too at large—O ! trembling heart,
Most sad are thy forebodings ; they are here——
Haste, Nima ; let us veil us from their view.
                           [they retire.

Enter MIAMI *and* GRIMOSCO.

Grim. Be satisfied ; I cannot fail—hither the
king will soon come. This deep shade have I chos-
en for our place of meeting. Hush ! he comes.
Retire, and judge if Grimosco have vainly boasted—
away !
                          [Miami retires.

Enter POWHATAN.

Pow. Now, priest, I attend the summons of thy
voice.
Grim. So you consult your safety, for 'tis the
voice of warning.
Pow. Of what would you warn me ?
Grim. Danger.
Pow. From whom ?
Grim. Your enemies.
Pow. Old man, these have I conquered.
Grim. The English still exist.
Pow. The English !
Grim. The nobler beast of the forest issues boldly
from his den, and the spear of the powerful pierces
his heart. The deadly adder lurks in his covert till
the unwary footstep approach him.
Pow. I see no adder near me.
Grim. No, for thine eyes rest only on the flowers
under which he glides.
Pow. Away, thy sight is dimmed by the shadows
of age.
Grim. King, for forty winters hast thou heard the
voice of counsel from my lips, and never did its
sound deceive thee ; never did my tongue raise the
war cry, and the foe appeared not. Be warned then
to beware the white man. He has fixed his ser-
pent eye upon you, and, like the charmed bird, you
flutter each moment nearer to the jaw of death.
Pow. How, Grimosco ?
Grim. Do you want proof of the white man's ha-
tred to the red ? Follow him along the bay ; count

the kings he has conquered, and the nations that his
sword has made extinct.
Pow. Like a warrior he subdued them, for the
chain of friendship bound them not to each other.
The white man is brave as Aresqui ; and can the
brave be treacherous ?
Grim. Like the red feather of the flamingo is
craft, the brightest plume that graces the warrior's
brow. Are not your people brave ? Yet does the
friendly tree shield them while the hatchet is thrown.
Who doubts the courage of Powhatan ? Yet has the
eye of darkness seen Powhatan steal to the surprise
of the foe.
Pow. Ha ! priest, thy words are true. I will be
satisfied. Even now I received a swift messenger
from my son : to day he will conduct the English to
my banquet. I will demand of him if he be the
friend of Powhatan.
Grim. Yes ; but demand it of him as thou draw-
est thy reeking hatchet from his cleft head. *(king
starts)* The despoilers of our land must die !
Pow. What red man can give his eye-ball the
glare of defiance when the white chief is nigh ? He
who stood alone amidst seven hundred foes, and,
while he spurned their king to the ground, dared
them to shoot their arrows ; who will say to him,
" White man, I am thine enemy ?" No one. My
chiefs would be children before him.
Grim. The valour of thy chiefs may slumber, but
the craft of thy priest shall watch. When the
English sit at that banquet from which they shall
never rise ; when their eyes read nothing but
friendship in thy looks, there shall hang a hatchet

over each victim head, which, at the silent signal of
Grimosco——
Pow. Forbear, counsellor of death ! Powhatan
cannot betray those who have vanquished his enemies ; who are his friends, his brothers.
Grim. Impious ! Can the enemies of your God
be your friends ? Can the children of another parent
be your brethren ? You are deaf to the counsellor :
'tis your priest now speaks. I have heard the angry voice of the Spirit you have offended ; offended
by your mercy to his enemies. Dreadful was his
voice ; fearful were his words. Avert his wrath, or
thou art condemned ; and the white men are the mi-
nisters of his vengeance.
Pow. Priest !
Grim. From the face of the waters will he send
them, in mighty tribes, and our shores will scarce
give space for their footsteps. Powhatan will fly before them ; his beloved child, his wives, all that is
dear to him, he will leave behind. Powhatan will
fly ; but whither ? which of his tributary kings will
shelter him ? Not one. Already they cry, " Powhatan is ruled by the white ; we will no longer be
the slaves of a slave !"
Pow. Ha !
Grim. Despoiled of his crown, Powhatan will be
hunted from the land of his ancestors. To strange
woods will the fugitive be pursued by the Spirit
whom he has angered——
Pow. O dreadful !
Grim. And at last, when the angel of death obeys
his call of anguish, whither will go his condemned
soul ? Not to the fair forests, where his brave fa-

thers are. O! never will Powhatan clasp the dear ones who have gone before him. His exiled, solitary spirit will for ever howl on the barren heath where the wings of darkness rest. No ray of hope shall visit him; eternal will be his night of despair.

Pow. Forbear, forbear! O, priest, teach me to avert the dreadful doom.

Grim. Let the white men be slaughtered.

Pow. The angry Spirit shall be appeased. Come.
[*exit.*

Grim. Thy priest will follow thee.

Enter MIAMI.

Mi. Excellent Grimosco! Thy breath, priest, is a deadly pestilence, and hosts fall before it. Yet—still is Miami a captive.

Grim. Fear not. Before Powhatan reach Werocomoco thou shalt be free. Come.

Mi. O, my soul hungers for the banquet; for then shall Miami feast on the heart of his rival!
[*exeunt with savage triumph.*

Music. The PRINCESS *rushes forward, terror depicted in her face. After running alternately to to each side, and stopping undetermined and bewildered, speaks.*

Prs. O whither shall I fly? what course pursue?
At Werocomoco, my phrenzied looks
Would sure betray me. What if hence I haste?
I may o'ertake my lover, or encounter

My brother and his friends. Away, my Nima!
[*exit Nima.*
O holy Spirit! thou whom my dear lover
Has taught me to adore and think most merciful,
Wing with thy lightning's speed my flying feet!
[*music. Exit Princess.*

SCENE III.—*Near Jamestown.*

Enter LARRY, *and* KATE *as a page.*

Lar. Nine ships, five hundred men, and a lord governor! Och! St. Patrick's blessing be upon them; they'll make this land flow with buttermilk like green Erin. What say you, master page, isn't this a nice neat patch to plant potatoes—I mean, to plant a nation in?

Kate. There's but one better.

Lar. And which might that be?

Kate. E'en little green Erin that you spoke of.

Lar. And were you ever—och, give me your fist—were you ever in Ireland?

Kate. It's there I was born—

Lar. I saw its bloom on your cheek.

Kate. And bred.

Lar. I saw it in your manners.

Kate. O, your servant, sir. (*bows*) And there, too, I fell in love.

Lar. And, by the powers, so did I; and if a man don't fall into one of the beautiful bogs that Cupid has digged there, faith he may stand without tumbling, though he runs over all the world beside. Och, the creatures, I can see them now—

Kate. Such sparkling eyes—

Lar. Rosy cheeks—

Kate. Pouting lips—

Lar. Tinder hearts! Och, sweet Ireland!

Kate. Ay, it was there that I fixed my affections after all my wanderings.

SONG—*Kate.*

Young Edward, through many a distant place,
  Had wandering pass'd, a thoughtless ranger;
And, cheer'd by a smile from beauty's face,
  Had laugh'd at the frowning face of danger.
      Fearless Ned,
      Careless Ned,
Never with foreign dames was a stranger;
      And huff,
      Bluff,
He laugh'd at the frowning face of danger.

But journeying on to his native place,
  Through Ballinamoné pass'd the stranger;
Where, fix'd by the charms of Katy's face,
  He swore he'd no longer be a ranger.
      Pretty Kate,
      Witty Kate,
Vow'd that no time could ever change her;
      And kiss,
      Bliss,
O, she hugg'd to her heart the welcome stranger.

Lar. How's that? Ballinamone, Kate, did you say, Kate?

Kate. Ay, Katy Maclure; as neat a little wanton tit—

Lar. My wife a wanton tit!—Hark ye, master Whipper-snapper, do you pretend—

Kate. Pretend! No, faith, sir, I scorn to *pretend*, sir; I am above boasting of ladies' favours, unless I receive 'em. Pretend, quotha!

Lar. Fire and faggots! Favours!—

Kate. You seem to know the girl, mister—a—

Lar. Know her! she's my wife.

Kate. Your wife! Ridiculous! I thought, by your pother, that she had been *your friend's wife,* or your mistress. Hark ye, mister—a—cuckoo—

Lar. Cuckoo!

Kate. Your ear. Your wife loved me as she did herself.

Lar. She did?

Kate. Couldn't live without me; all day we were together.

Lar. You were!

Kate. As I'm a cavalier; and all night—we lay—

Lar. How?

Kate. How! why, close as two twin potatoes; in the same bed, egad!

Lar. Tunder and turf! I'll split you from the coxcomb to the——

Kate. Ay, do split the twin potatoe asunder, do.
[*discovers herself.*

Lar. It is—no—what! Och, is it nobody but yourself? O, my darling!—(*catches her in his arms.*) And so—But how did you?—And where—and what——O, boderation! (*kisses*) And how d'ye do? and how's your mother? and the pigs and praties, and——kiss me, Kate (*kiss*).

Kate. So; now may I speak?

Lar. Ay, do be telling me—but stop every now

and then, that I may point your story with a grammatical kiss.

Kate. O, hang it! you'll be for putting nothing but periods to my discourse.

Lar. Faith, and I should be for counting—(*kisses*)—four.—Arrah! there, then; I've done with that sentence.

Kate. You remember what caused me to stay behind, when you embarked for America?

Lar. Ay, 'twas because of your old sick mother. And how does the good lady? (*Kate weeps*) Ah! well, Heaven rest her soul.—Cheerly, cheerly. To be sure, I can't give *you* a mother; but I tell you what I'll do, I'll give your children one; and that's the same thing, you know. So, kiss me, Kate. Cheerly.

Kate. One day, as I sat desolate in my cottage, a carriage broke down near it, from which a young lady was thrown with great violence. My humble cabin received her, and I attended her till she was able to resume her journey.

Lar. My kind Kate!

Kate. The sweet young lady promised me her protection, and pressed me to go with her. So, having no mother—nor Larry to take care of——

Lar. You let the pigs and praties take care of themselves.

Kate. I placed an honest, poor neighbour in my cottage, and followed the fortunes of my mistress—and—oh Larry, such an angel!

Lar. But where is she?

Kate. Here, in Virginia.

Lar. Here?

Kate. Ay, but that's a secret.

Lar. Oh! is it so? that's the reason then you won't tell it me.

GERALDINE, *as a page, and* WALTER *appear behind.*

Kate. That's she.

Lar. Where?

Kate. There.

Lar. Bother! I see no one but a silken cloaked spark, and our Wat; devil a petticoat!

Kate. That spark is my mistress.

Lar. Be asy. Are you sure you arn't his mistress?

Kate. Tut, now you've got the twin potatoes in your head.

Lar. Twins they must be, if any, for faith I hav'n't had a *single* potatoe in my head this many a long day. But come, my Kate, tell me how you and your mistress happened to jump into—

Kate. Step aside then.

Lar. Have with you, my dapper page.

[*they retire.*

Geraldine and Walter advance.

Ger. You know this Percy, then?

Wal.   Know him! O yes!
He makes this wild wood, here, a past'ral grove.
He is a love-lorn shepherd; an Orlando,
Carving love-rhymes and cyphers on the trees,
And warbling dying ditties of a lady
He calls false Geraldine.

Ger.   O my dear Percy!
How has one sad mistake marr'd both our joys! [*aside.*

Wal. Yet, though a shepherd, he can wield a sword
As easy as a crook.

Ger.   Oh! he is brave.

Wal. As Julius Cæsar, sir, or Hercules;
Or any other hero that you will,
Except our captain.

Ger.   Is your captain, then,
Without his peer?

Wal.   Ay, marry is he, sir,
Sans equal in this world. I've follow'd him
Half o'er the globe, and seen him do such deeds!
His shield is blazon'd with three Turkish heads.

Ger. Well, sir.

Wal.   And I, boy, saw him win the arms:
O 'twas the bravest act!

Ger.   Prithee, recount it.

Wal. It was at Regal, close beleaguer'd then
By the duke Sigismund of Transylvania,
Our captain's general. One day, from the gate
There issued a gigantic mussulman,
And threw his gauntlet down upon the ground,
Daring our christian knights to single combat.
It was our captain, sir, pick'd up the glove,
And scarce the trump had sounded to the onset,
When the Turk Turbisha had lost his head.
His brother, fierce Grualdo, enter'd next,
But left the lists sans life or turban too.
Last came black Bonamolgro, and he paid
The same dear forfeit for the same attempt.
And now my master, like a gallant knight,

His sabre studded o'er with ruby gems,
Prick'd on his prancing courser round the field,
In vain inviting fresh assailants; while
The beauteous dames of Regal, who, in throngs
Lean'd o'er the rampart to behold the tourney,
Threw show'rs of scarfs and favours from the wall,
And wav'd their hands, and bid swift Mercuries
Post from their eyes with messages of love;
While manly modesty and graceful duty
Wav'd on his snowy plume, and, as he rode,
Bow'd down his casque unto the saddle bow.

Ger. It was a deed of valour, and you've dress'd it
In well-beseeming terms. And yet, methinks,
I wonder at the ladies' strange delight;
And think the spectacle might better suit
An audience of warriors than of women.
I'm sure I should have shudder'd—that is, sir,
If I were woman.

Wal.   Cry your mercy, page;
Were you a woman, you would love the brave.
You're yet but boy; you'll know the truth of this,
When father Time writes man upon your chin.

Ger. No doubt I shall, sir, when I get a beard.

Wal. My master, boy, has made it chrystal clear:
Be but a Mars, and you shall have your Venus.

SONG—*Walter.*

Captain Smith is a man of might,
In Venus' soft wars or in Mars' bloody fight:
For of widow, or wife, or of damsel bright,
 A bold blade, you know, is all the dandy.

One day his sword he drew,
And a score of Turks he slew;
    When done his toil,
    He snatch'd the spoil,
    And, as a part,
    The gentle heart
Of the lovely lady Tragabizandy.

Captain Smith trod the Tartar land;
While before him, in terror, fled the turban'd band,
With his good broad-sword, that he whirl'd in his hand,
    To a three-tail'd bashaw he gave a pat—a.
    The bashaw, in alarm,
    Turn'd tails, and fled his arm.
        But face to face,
        With lovely grace,
        In all her charms,
        Rush'd to his arms
The beautiful lady Calamata.

Captain Smith, from the foaming seas,
From pirates, and shipwreck, and miseries,
In a French lady's arms found a haven of ease;
    Her name—pshaw! from memory quite gone 't has.
    And on this savage shore,
    Where his faulchion stream'd with gore,
        His noble heart
        The savage dart
        Had quiver'd through;
        But swifter flew
To his heart the pretty princess Pocahontas.
                                        [exit Walter.

                    Enter KATE.

Ger. Now, brother page—
    Kate.   Dear mistress, I have found
My faithful Larry.

    Ger.   Happy girl! and I
Hope soon to meet my heart's dear lord, my Percy.
Hist! the lord governor——
    Kate.   He little thinks
Who is the page he loves so——
    Ger.   Silence.
    Kate.   Mum.

            Enter DELAWAR, WALTER, LARRY, *&c.*

    Del. Each noble act of his that you recite
Challenges all my wonder and applause.
Your captain is a brave one; and I long
To press the hero's hand. But look, my friends,
What female's this, who, like the swift Camilla,
On airy step flies hitherward?
    Wal.   My lord,
This is the lovely princess you have heard of;
Our infant colony's best patroness;
Nay, sir, its foster-mother.
    Del.   Mark how wild——

Music. The PRINCESS *enters, with wild anxiety in
her looks; searches eagerly around for Smith
and Rolfe.*

    Del. Whom do you look for, lady?
    Prs.   They are gone!
Gone to be slaughter'd!
    Wal.   If you seek our captain,
He has departed for your father's banquet.
    Prs. Then they have met, and they will both be
        lost,

My lover and my friend. O! faithless path,
That led me from my lover! Strangers, fly!
If you're the white man's friends——
    Del.   Lady, we are.
    Prs. Then fly to save them from destruction!
    Del.   How?
    Prs. Inquire not; speak not; treachery and
        death
Await them at the banquet.
    Del.   Haste, my friends,
Give order for immediate departure.
    Prs. E'en now perhaps they bleed! O lover!
        brother!
Fly, strangers, fly!

    Music. Drum beats; a bustle; scene closes.

SCENE IV. *At Werocomoco; banquet.* SMITH,
ROLFE, PERCY, NANTAQUAS, POWHATAN, *&c.,*
seated. GRIMOSCO, MIAMI, *and a number of
Indians attending.*

    Pow. White warriors, this is the feast of peace,
and yet you wear your arms. Will not my friends
lay by their warlike weapons? They fright our
fearful people.
    Sm. Our swords are part of our apparel, king;
Nor need your people fear them. They shall
        rest
Peaceful within their scabbards, if Powhatan
Call them not forth, with voice of enmity.
    Pow. O that can never be! feast then in peace,
Children and friends——

Leaves his place and comes forward to Grimosco.

O priest! my soul is afraid it will be stained with
dishonour.
    Grim. Away! the Great Spirit commands you.
Resume your seat; hold the white men in discourse; I will but thrice wave my hand, and your
foes are dead. (*King resumes his seat*) (*to Miami*)
Now, prince, has the hour of vengeance arrived.
    Pow. (*with a faltering voice*) Think not, white
men, that Powhatan wants the knowledge to prize
your friendship. Powhatan has seen three gene-
rations pass away; and his locks of age do not
float upon the temples of folly.

*Grimosco waves his hand: the Indians steal be-
hind the English, Miami behind Rolfe. King proceeds.*

If a leaf but fall in the forest, my people cry out
with terror, "hark! the white warrior comes!"
Chief, thou art terrible as an enemy, and Powhatan knows the value of thy friendship.

*Grimosco waves his hand again; the Indians seize
their tomahawks, and prepare to strike. King
goes on.*

Think not, therefore, Powhatan can attempt to
deceive thee——

*The king's voice trembles; he stops, unable to proceed.
The Indians' eyes are fixed on Grimosco, waiting
for the last signal. At this moment the* PRINCESS
rushes in.

Prs. Treachery to the white men!

At the same instant, drum and trumpet without. Music. The English seize the uplifted arms of the Indians, and form a tableau, as enter DELAWAR and his party. After the music, the soldiers take charge of the Indians. Pocahontas flies to the arms of Rolfe.

Nan. Oh father!

       [*Powhatan is transfixed with confusion.*

Sm.   Wretched king! what fiend could urge you?

Pow. Shame ties the tongue of Powhatan. Ask of that fiend-like priest, how, to please the angry Spirit, I was to massacre my friends.

Sm. Holy Religion! still beneath the veil Of sacred piety what crimes lie hid! Bear hence that monster. Thou ferocious prince——

Mi. Miami's tortures shall not feast your eyes!

       [*stabbing himself.*

Sm. Rash youth, thou mightst have liv'd——

Mi. Liv'd! man, look there!

       [*pointing to Rolfe and princess. He is borne off.*

Pow. Oh, if the false Powhatan might——

Sm.   No more. Wiser than thou have been the dupes of priest-hood. Your hand. The father of this gen'rous pair I cannot chuse but love. My noble lord, I pray you pardon my scant courtesy And sluggish duty, which so tardy-paced Do greet your new arrival——

Del.   Valiant captain! Virtue-ennobled sir, a hero's heart

Will make mine proud by its most near acquain-tance.   [*embrace.*

Sm. Your coming was most opportune, my lord. One moment more——

Del.   Nay, not to us the praise. Behold the brilliant star that led us on.

Sm. Oh! blest is still its kindly influence! Could a rough soldier play the courtier, lady, His practis'd tongue might grace thy various goodness, With proper phrase of thanks; but oh! reward thee! Heaven only can——

Prs.   And has, my brother. See! I have its richest gift.   [*turning to Rolfe.*

Rol.   My dearest love!

Sm. Her brother, sir, and worthy of that name.

Introduces Nantaquas to Delawar; Percy and Geraldine, who had been conversing, advance.

Per. You tell me wonders.

Ger.   But not miracles. Being near the uncle, sir, I knew the lady.

Per. And was I then deceived?

Del.   What, gentle Percy! Young man, 'twas not well done, in idle pique, To wound the heart that lov'd you.

Per.   O sir! speak! My Geraldine, your niece, is she not married?

Del. Nor like to be; poor wench, but to her grave, If mourning for false lovers break maids' hearts.

Per. Was she then true? O madman! ideot! To let the feeble breath of empty rumour Drive me from heavenly happiness!

Del.   Poor girl! She fain would have embark'd with me.

Per.   Ah, sir! Why did she not?

Del.   Marry sir, I forbade her: The rough voyage would have shook her slender health To dissolution.

Ger. Pardon, sir; not so——

Del. How now, pert page?

Ger.   For here she is, my lord. And the rough voyage has giv'n her a new life.

Per. My Geraldine!

Del.   My niece! O, brazenface! Approach me not; fly from your uncle's anger; Fly to your husband's arms for shelter, hussey!

       [*Geraldine flies to Percy's embrace.*

Per. Oh! speechless transport! mute let me in-fold thee!

Del. (*to Kate*) And you, my little spark, per-haps your cloak Covers another duteous niece—or daughter. Speak, lady: for I see that title writ In crimson characters upon your cheek. Art of my blood?

Lar.   No, sir, she's of my flesh; Flesh of my flesh, my lord. Now, arrah, Kate, Don't blush. This goodly company all knows My flesh may wear the breeches, without scandal.

Wal. Listen not, Alice, to his sophistry. Sir, if our good wives learn this argument, They'll logically pluck away our——

Al.   Tut: Fear ye not that; for when a woman would, She'll draw them on without a rule of reason.

Del. Methinks 'tis pairing time among the tur-tles. Who have we here?

Robin and Nima come forward.

Rob. A pair of pigeons, sir; or rather a robin and a dove. A wild thing, sir, that I caught in the wood here. But when I have clipt her wings, and tamed her, I hope (without offence to this good company) that we shall bill without biting more than our neighbours.

Sm. Joy to ye, gentle lovers; joy to all; A goodly circle, and a fair. Methinks Wild Nature smooths apace her savage frown, Moulding her features to a social smile. Now flies my hope-wing'd fancy o'er the gulf That lies between us and the aftertime, When this fine portion of the globe shall teem With civiliz'd society; when arts, And industry, and elegance shall reign, As the shrill war-cry of the savage man Yields to the jocund shepherd's roundelay. Oh, enviable country! thus disjoin'd From old licentious Europe! may'st thou rise, Free from those bonds which fraud and superstition In barbarous ages have enchain'd *her* with;

Bidding the antique world with wonder view
A great, yet virtuous empire in the west !

FINALE.

Freedom, on the western shore
   Float thy banner o'er the brave ;
Plenty, here thy blessings pour ;
   Peace, thy olive sceptre wave !

Percy, Walter, &c.   Fire-eyed Valour, guard the land ;
   Here uprear thy fearless crest ;
Prs. Kate, Al. &c.   Love, diffuse thy influence bland
   O'er the regions of the west.

Chorus.   Freedom, &c.

Larry.   Hither, lassie, frank and pretty,
   Come and live without formality.
Thou, in English christen'd Pity,
   But call'd, in Irish, Hospitality.

Chorus.   Freedom, &c.

THE END.

THE INDIAN PRINCESS

Score

THE
INDIAN PRINCESS,
OR
La Belle Sauvage.

An Operatic Melo Drame,

IN THREE ACTS.

Performed at the

New Theatre Philadelphia.

Written by M.ʳ J. N. Barker.

The Music by

JOHN BRAY.

Copy Right Secured. ———————————— Price 3 Dollars.

PHILADELPHIA. Published by G. E. BLAKE N.º 1 S 3.ᵈ Street.

OVERTURE,

4

For.

For.

Ria.

For:

Indian Princess.

Indian Princess

Indian Princees.

Chorus of Adventurers.

ALLEGRO.

Solo, then repeat in Chorus.

Jolly comrades join the glee,

Chorus it right cheeri . ly, Jolly Comrades join the glee, Chorus it right cheerily,

1st time

2d time

cheerily. For the tem _ pest's roar, Is heard no

Indian Princess.

more, But gaily, gaily we tread the wish'd for

Vio

shore, We tread the wish'd for Shore - - - - - - - - - - - - - - -

Jolly Comrades join the glee, Chorus it right cheeri-ly, Jolly Comrades

join the glee, Chorus it right cheerily, For past are the perils of the blust'ring

sea, For past are the perils of the blust'ring sea, Of the blust'ring sea, Of the

Pia.   For:

blust'ring sea, Of the blust'ring sea.

Indian Princess.

Ever, ever cheery!

A Favorite Song,

Sung by Mrs Mills,

In the New Operatic Melo Drame of

THE INDIAN PRINCESS

or

La Belle Sauvage,

Copy Right Secured.

Composed by IOHN BRAY.

ANDANTINO

AFFETUOSO.

ALICE

In this

wild wood will I range, Listen, listen dear, Nor sigh for towns so

For: P.a.

fine, to change, This Forest, forest drear: Toil and danger I'll despise,

Indian Princess.

Indian Princess.

And while the wind blow'd & Kate sigh'd might & main, Drops from the black skies fell, &

from her black eyes Och! how I was soak'd with her tears and the rain,

(SPEAKS)

And then she gave me this butiful keep_sake (shews a pair of large Scissors) which if ever I part with, may a Taylor clip me in two with his big shears — Och! when Katty took you in hand, how nicely did you snip and snap my bushy, carrotty locks — and now you're cutting the hairs of my heart to pieces you tieves you,

(SINGS)

Och! Hubbaboo! Gramachree! Hone!

2.

When I went in the Garden each bush seem'd to sigh,
Becase I was going — and nod me "good bye"
Each stem hung it's head, drooping, bent like a bow,
With the weight of the water, or else of it's woe:
And while sorrow or wind laid some flat on the ground,
Drops of rain, or of grief,
Fell from every leaf,
'Till I thought in a big show'r of tears I was drown'd.

(SPEAKS)

And then each bush and leaf seem'd to sigh and say "don't forget us Larry," "I went" said I — "But arrah! take something for remembrance" said they — and then I dug up this neat Jewel (shews a potatoe) — You're a little wither'd to be sure, but if ever I forget your respectable family, or your delightful dwelling place — may I never again see any of your beautiful brothers and plump sisters — Och! my darling if you had come hot from the hand of Katty, how my mouth would have water'd at ye — Now you de_vils, you bring the water into my eyes.

(SINGS)

Och! Hubbaboo! Gramachree! Hone!

Indian Princess

Indian Girls arranging Flowers.

Pocohontas enters from the woods.

Indians stealing after Smith.

Indian Princess.

Indians fighting with Smith.

Nantaquas rushes out after Indians.

Indian Princess.

DIALOGUE QUARTETTO

Sung by
Mess.rs Jefferson. Webster. Bray & M.rs Mills.

ALLEGRO.

ROBIN

VOICE.

Mistress Alice say___ Walters far a_way, Pretty Alice!

PIANO

FORTE.

Nay now prithee pray, Shall we Alice ha? Mistress Alice!

ALICE

Master Robin, nay___ Prithee go your way, Sau_cy Robin!

If you longer stay, You may rue the day, Master Robin.

Indian Princess.

Finale to First Act.

Sung by Adventurers.

ALLEGRO.

1st time Pia. 2nd Forte.

Soprano 1no

Now crimson sinks the setting sun, And our tasks are fairly done, Jolly comrades home to bed &

2nd

Now crimson sinks the setting sun, And our tasks are fairly done, Jolly comrades home to bed &

Basso

Now crimson sinks the setting sun, And our tasks are fairly done, Jolly comrades home to bed &

Piano

Forte.

taste the sweets by labour shed.   Let his poppy seal your eyes 'Till another day arise,

taste the sweets by labour shed.

taste the sweets by labour shed.   Let his poppy seal your eyes 'Till another day arise,

Indian Princess.

taste the sweets by labour shed.   Jolly comrades home to bed, Taste the sweets by labour

taste the sweets by labour shed.   Jolly comrades home to bed, Taste the sweets by labour

taste the sweets by labour shed.   Jolly comrades home to bed, Taste the sweets by labour

shed, Jolly comrades home to bed, Taste the sweets by labour shed, by   la_bour   shed, by

shed, Jolly comrades home to bed, Taste the sweets by labour shed, by   la_bour   shed, by

shed, Jolly comrades home to bed, Taste the sweets by labour shed, by   la_bour   shed, by

labour   shed, by   labour   shed, by   la_bour   shed, labour shed, labour shed.

labour   shed, by   labour   shed, by   la_bour   shed, labour shed, labour shed.

labour   shed, by   labour   shed, by   la_bour   shed, labour shed, labour shed.

Indian Princess.

Smith brought in prisoner.

Smith is led to the Block.

The Princess leads Smith to the throne.

She supplicates the King for his pardon.

Smith is pardoned — general joy diffused.

Indian Princess.

FAIR GERALDINE,

A favorite Song,

Sung by Mr. Charnock in the

New Operatic MeloDrame of the

INDIAN PRINCESS

or

La Belle Sauvage.

Composed by JOHN BRAY.

Copy Right Secured.

PERCY.

Fair Ge_ral_dine each charm of spring possess'd, Her cheeks glow'd

with the Rose and Lilly's strife, Her breath was per_fume, and each

win..ter'd breast   Felt that her sunny eyes beam'd light and

life,   Felt that her sunny eyes, Her eyes beam'd light and life.

2nd VERSE.

A-las! that in a

form of blooming May, The mind should April's changeful liv'ry wear, But

Ah! like April smiling, smiling to be-tray,   Is Geraldine as

false   as   she   is   fair,   Is Geraldine as   false,   as

false as she is fair.

Indian Princess.

Without a penny of money!

A favorite GLEE for three Voices
Arranged with an Accompaniment for
Two Performers on one Piano Forte
Sung by
Mess.rs Webster, Jefferson & Bray,
in the New Operatic Melo Drame of the
Indian Princess or La Belle Sauvage.
Composed by John Bray.

Indian Princess.

V.S.

penny of mo - - - ney, With - - out a penny, with - out a

penny of mo - - - ney, With - - out a penny, with - out a

penny of mo - - - ney, With - - out a penny, with - out a

penny, And have cross'd thrice a thou - sand miles of sea, With - - out a

penny, And have cross'd thrice a thou - sand miles of sea, With - - out a

penny, And have cross'd thrice a thou - sand miles of sea, With - out a

Indian Princess.

2.

We three good fellows be,
Who would run like the devil from Indians three,
We never admir'd their bowmandry,
Oh give us whole skins for our money,

        Whole skins for our money &c.

3.

We three merry men be,
Who gaily will chaunt our Ancient Glee,
Tho' a lass or a glass in this wild Country
Can't be had, or for love or for money,

        For love or for money &c.

Indian Princess.

Smith, Nantaquas &c. take leave of the Princess.

Rolfe leaves her.

Indians assemble & prepare for war.

Indian Princess.

Indian Princess.

Indian Princess.

Dance and March.

Act 3d
Bustle — Fleet discovered at a distance.

Rolfe takes leave of the Princess.

Indian Princess.

When the Midnight of Absence

A favorite Song.

Sung by Mrs. Wilmot, in the
New Operatic Melo Drame of the

INDIAN PRINCESS

(or)

La Belle Sauvage.

Composed by John Bray.

Copy Right Secured.

POCOHONTAS.

When the midnight of absence the day scene per_

_vading, Dis_tills it's chill dew o'er the bo_som of love, How fast then the

gay tints of nature seem fading, How harsh seems the music of joy in the

grove And the tender flower bends till re_turn of the light, Steep'd in

tear drops that fall from the eye of the night

Oboes.

34

ALLEGRETTO

But ah! when the lov'd one appears, Like the Sun a bright day to impart, To

kiss off those envious tears, To gain a new warmth to the heart. But

ah! when the lov'd one appears, Like the Sun a bright day to impart, To kiss off those envious

tears, To give a new warmth to the heart, To kiss off those envious tears, To

give a new warmth to the heart.

ALLEGRETTO.

Soon the flowret seeming dead, Raises up it's blushing head,

Raises up it's blushing head, Glows again the heart of love, Laughs again the

Indian Princees.

joyful grove. And again the mock bird's throat,

Trolls the sweetly varying note, And trols the sweetly

varying note, And trolls the sweetly varying note

ANDANTE.

But ah! when dark abscence the day scene per _ vad _ ing, Dis

_tills it's chill dew o'er the bosom of love, O fast then the gay tints of

nature seem fading, O harsh seems the music of joy in the grove, of

ad lib. Dem

joy in the grove, of joy in the grove.

Indian Princess.

CARELESS NED!

A favorite Song,

Sung by Miss Hunt! in the
New Operatic Melo Drame of the

INDIAN PRINCESS

or

La Belle Sauvage!

Composed by

JOHN BRAY.

Copy Right Secured.

MODERATO.

KATE.

Young Edward thro' many a distant place, Had wand'ring past a

thoughtless ranger And cheer'd by a smile from beauty's face, Had laugh'd at the

frowning face of danger, Fearless Ned, Careless Ned,

Never with foreign dames was a stranger, But huff! bluff! huff! bluff! He

laugh'd at the frowning face of danger, He laugh'd at the frowning face of danger, He

laugh'd at the frowning face of danger.

2.

But journeying on to his native place,
Thro' Ballinamona pass'd the stranger,
Wher fixt by the charms of Katty's face,
He swore he'd no longer be a ranger.
Pretty Kate _ Witty Kate _
Vow'd that **no time** should ever change her,
And Kiss _ Bliss

CAPTAIN SMITH.

A favorite Song,

in the New Operatic Melo Drame of the

INDIAN PRINCESS

or

La Belle Sauvage

Composed and Sung by

JOHN BRAY.

Copy Right Secured.

MAESTOSO

WALTER.

Captain Smith is a man of night, In Venus soft wars or in Mars bloody fight, And of widow or wife or of damsel bright, A bold blade you know is all the dandy. One day his sword he drew, And a score of Turks he slew, When done his toil, He snatch'd the spoil, And as a part, The gentle heart Of the lovely lady Tragabi-

ad lib.　Tempo

randy, Oh the lovely la_dy, The la_dy Tra_ga_bi_

randy. And as a part, He stole the heart, Of the lovely lady Tragabi

_randy.

2.

Captain Smith, trod the Tartar land,
While before him, in terror fled the turban'd band,
With his good broad sword that he whirld in his hand.
  To a three tail'd Bashaw he gave a pat _ d
      The Bashaw in alarm,
      Turn'd tails and fled his arm;
      But face to face,
      With blooming grace,
      In all her charms,
      Rush'd to his arms,
The beautiful Lady Calamata.
      Oh the lovely &c.&c.

3.

Captain Smith, from the foaming seas,
From pirates, and shipwreck, and miseries,
In a french lady's arms found a haven of ease;
  Her name _ psha! from memory quite gone 't has_
      And on this savage shore,
      Where his faulchion stream'd with gore,
      The Indian dart,
      His noble heart,
      Had quiver'd through,
      But swifter flew
To his heart, the pretty Princess Pocohontas
      Oh the pretty Princess &c.

Delawar and soldiers set out for the banquet.

The Princess rushes in _ Soldiers secure the Indians.

Indian Princess.

ALLEGRO.

CHORUS. *Ria.*

Freedom on the western shore, Float thy banner o'er the brave, Plenty all thy blessings pour, Peace thy olive septre wave.

For. Freedom on the Western shore, Float thy banner o'er the brave, Plenty all thy

WALTER, PERCY &c.

blessings pour, Peace thy olive sceptre wave. Fire ey'd valour guard the land,

LADIES.

Here uprear thy rugged crest, Love diffuse thy influence bland, O'er the regions

DAL SEGNO.

Oboe

of the west - - - - - - - - - -

Indian Princess.

LARRY

Hither lassie frank and pretty, Hither come wit - out formale - ty,

Thou, in English christen'd pity, But in Irish hos - pi - ta - li - ty.

CHORUS. *Pia.*

Freedom on the western shore, Float thy banner o'er the brave, Plenty all thy

For:

blessings pour, Peace thy olive sceptre wave, Freedom on thy western shore,

Float thy banner o'er the brave, Plenty all thy blessings pour,

Peace thy olive sceptre wave, Peace thy olive sceptre, wave,

Peace thy olive sceptre wave.

Indian Princess.   FINIS